THE PROMISE BORN

JESSICA CAGE

AUTOGRAPH PAGE

CONTENTS

CHAPTER 1

There was nothing more annoying than the thunderous sound of dragon wings drowning out the sweet tune of the morning birds. Each day started the same. I would stand beneath the sun, a cup of gem leaf tea in hand, and clear my mind. Most mornings, I woke up with rampant thoughts and that was the only way to get myself ready for another day running my shop.

Simple Delights. That was the name hanging over the door. Opening the shop had been a dream of mine since I was a small girl. Of course, I had to fight my mother on the idea. But she wasn't around to stop me anymore. So, I could do whatever I wanted to do. And the first chance I got, I ran to a new town and started working on my dreams.

Clayhorn had taken me in when I stumbled into its borders, an outsider with nothing but recipes and stubbornness. The one who'd shown up and swooned the locals with her delicacies. I fed the townsfolk and kept to myself. I'd created a refuge for myself, a quiet corner where I could escape the noise and worries of the world. That meant keeping out of business that wasn't my own. And the large convoy of dragons flying ahead was just that. None of my business.

But even I couldn't ignore the dragons. The sight of them flying ahead ignited a burning curiosity within me, a feeling both thrilling and unsettling.

I squinted my eyes against the rays of sunlight to see the signs of opulence hanging from the dragon and the device fastened to it, signifying a rider. The only people who rode dragons anymore were the royals. The rest of us would shift and use our own wings to carry us across the land. Not the royals. They had to keep themselves presentable and shifting often got ugly. And how could a queen be dignified when her appearance was a mess?

Within minutes, the town's people came running out of their homes to watch the dragons. The Royal's special spot, the large grassy center near the center of town, was overgrown and full of weeds from neglect. I understood the excitement of the others. They wanted to see what would finally bring the royals our way.

The nagging curiosity propelled me. I wrapped a dark scarf around my head and joined the throng of people, their hushed whispers hinting at the surprise visitors. The air buzzed with the frustrated sighs and muttered complaints about unpaid taxes and fines. After all, that was the only reason the royals ever made an appearance. As long as taxes were paid, they didn't care about us. And even then, they normally sent the guards to handle the tax collections, not fly in themselves.

That was the way I liked it. It was why I chose the small town of Clayhorn as my new home. I didn't want too many eyes on me or my work.

"Kiala, even you're out to catch sight of the visitors," an aged voice called out to me.

I turned around and saw Mesi's familiar face, the first woman to ever taste my food and my most loyal customer.

"I figured it might be a big deal. They rarely come here," I answered the gray-haired old lady, who nodded and shuffled forward to join her friends.

From what I knew of the trio, they had been friends since they were kids. When they were old enough, they traveled the world together. They never married or had children, each choosing friendship over love. And when their wings grew tired, they chose Clayhorn as their home.

I was sure that if one passed, the others would soon follow. They were one soul in three vessels.

I listened to their chatter and laughter as I followed them into the growing crowd.

"I think that was the prince's dragon." Mesi looked at her friends and hooked her arms through theirs.

"Maybe he's here to find love." Margo, the redhead one who always wore too much perfume, blushed. "Wouldn't that be sweet? He's at that age, you know. "

"A royal coming here to find love is a ridiculous thought. Who would he find here that would ever be accepted by the royals? That would be a cruel joke to play." Soki, the dark-haired one, scoffed. "He's probably here to collect taxes."

"How could you say that?" Mesi sucked her teeth and glanced back at me. "There are plenty of quality eligible girls here. I'm sure one of them could catch his eye."

"Always the optimist with your head in the clouds." Soki fussed, and they all cackled.

"Well, you know, she could be right," Margo spoke again. "I hear the queen has been pressuring him to find a bride. Avin, who works in the castles, told me they are preparing to pass the torch. If they do, he'll at least need to have a love interest. I mean, they're still old-fashioned like that. If he doesn't have one, it shows weakness."

"A shame. And he is next in line now." Mesi's voice was suddenly heavy with sorrow. "His brother was a fine prince. He would have made an excellent king as well."

"Asante is fine as well, but from what I hear, his head is in the clouds. I don't think finding a wife is something that can fix that." Soki added. "But it is time. The king and queen have done a fine job ruling. They deserve to step down."

"A good woman can work miracles!" Mesi clapped. "But can she make a prince a king?"

"Are you applying for the position?" Soki poked her side. "Do you think you can make him a king?"

"If the prince would have me!" Mesi wiggled her hips. "It doesn't really matter what I think. Besides, with my bad knees and wrinkled neck, he won't be asking my opinion!"

The trio cackled as they shuffled forward, and Mesi glanced back at me once again. I waved shyly and fell back. There was something about the way she kept looking at me that made my stomach cramp. That fear of being found.

It was paranoia, nothing more.

We made it to the center of town in time to see the dragons all poised to let their riders down.

In Saldann, there were two types of dragons: those who could change their forms into a bipedal state, and those who were locked in dragon form that made it impossible for them to integrate with other populations. We all descended from them, but something changed the bloodlines, creating three branches. The Stagnant, the Fire, and my bloodline, the Ice.

Fire were shifters who produced fire, and Ice were the opposite. Stagnants could not shift and had no power of their own, but they did have a special *gift*: they could replicate the power of the rider. If an ice shifter rode a Stagnant, that Stagnant could then breathe the same ice as the rider. The same for the fire.

Royals always rode Stagnants. That never sat right with me.

These were our cousins, our family, and yet they were being treated as nothing more than mules.

I wondered how they felt.

Gone were the days when shifters and stagnant could still communicate with one another. Some say we lost the ability to. But I always thought they just stopped talking to us. Perhaps a sense of betrayal gnawed at them, keeping them from sharing their thoughts with us.

I pulled the scarf tighter around my head as, one by one, the members of the royal visitors appeared. A murmur spread across the crowd as we all waited to get a view of the most important person. Sure, guards and aides were nice to see, but aside from their attire, they did not differ from the people who gathered to see them.

I admired their appearance. They were all dressed in black leathers adorned with red and gold trimming. Simple and clean looks that echoed the taste of the queen. It was something I'd always admired about her: she didn't subscribe to the gaudy show of wealth often displayed by those in power.

Then it happened. The gasps erupted as he appeared. He stepped down from the shaded seat atop the dragon, his cape swaying around him as he moved. He was tall, with dark brown skin, broad shoulders, and full lips. Long braids hung down around his face, perfectly framing his strong jawline and wide nose.

The prince of Starwell.

Prince Asante was everything I had heard. The villagers' accounts of the man—his height, his build, his distinctive walk—were finally confirmed by my own observation. With each step, he straightened more, pushing his shoulders back and lifting his chin with pride. The corners of his lips lifted in a soft smile.

And then his eyes scanned the crowd, assessing the faces of the gathered.

While others swooned, I narrowed my gaze. Asante was handsome, but I could sense the air of arrogance under that soft smile. He was still from a royal bloodline after all, which meant he was inherently full of himself.

I waited for one of his aides to make an announcement. Tell us why they had come, but the prince skipped the typical formalities. Instead, flanked by guards and aides, he walked around the crowd and addressed only the elders while simply glancing at the women. He gave each woman an appraising look before moving on to the next.

The old women were right. He was there to find a mate. And the women were actively posing themselves to be seen by him.

And not just the available women. One woman I knew to be in a relationship with the local blacksmith. She had no shame as she pushed her breasts up and pursed her lips. Apparently, any man could lose the love of his life if the prince saw it fit.

Disgusted with the display, I turned to leave. I had no intention of being perceived or of being chosen by the prince. Marriage was not an option in my mind, and being anywhere near the royal family was the absolute last thing I wanted.

When I moved to flee, one of the cackling trio tumbled. If I didn't know better, I could have sworn she did it on purpose. Mesi looked me right in the eye and then her little body jerked toward me. As I lunged to catch her, she flailed her arms like a madwoman and knocked me over. I turned to catch myself, but after clutching for anything to disrupt the fall, I found myself face down on the ground with everyone staring at me. So much for not being seen.

I took several deep breaths to calm myself in the embarrassing moment before trying to get up.

Kneeling, I saw a gloved hand offered to help me up. Without questioning who it belonged to, I accepted the help. What I hadn't realized was that the long scarf I'd used to hide my face had shifted. The end of it snagged beneath my foot and as I stood, it ripped away. I panicked and tried to grab it but failed. Once again, the hand was there, picking up the discarded scarf to give to me.

"Here you go." The rich voice spoke as he returned my scarf.

"Thanks-," I paused as I looked up to see the face of the man I'd hoped to avoid.

"Are you alright?" he peered at me with an expression dripping with concern.

"Yes, thank you." I snatched my hand away from him as soon as I was on my feet, did a short curtsy, and turned to leave.

I didn't make it far before I heard him say the words that made my insides boil.

"That one will do." The prince's low voice announced.

Those misogynist words described not a thing that could be purchased, but a woman who had every right to deny whatever it was he intended with that statement. I could have continued to walk and ignore it. I could have minded my business. But not this time. Instead, I turned around to find the prince.

He spoke to a short aide who stood next to him. The man was older, with gray whiskers sprouting from his face. He had two golden talons pinned at this chest. The markers of someone the royals deemed important.

While the prince didn't look at me as he made his remarks, he pointed at me. "She looks good enough to get my mother off my back."

The aide, eyes sharp and alert, noticed me before the prince.

"Sir," the aide said, his nose wrinkling in disgust as he eyed the dirt now covering my clothing.

"My mother wants me to marry. I will," the prince spoke, oblivious to the fact I was staring right at him. "But I will choose who I spend my life with. She won't force me into being with someone I don't want."

"But she is... beneath you," the aide said, making full eye contact with me.

"She will serve her purpose. That's all that matters." The prince answered, but there was a softness to his tone that betrayed his dismissive words. Were there other motives behind his choice?

"Excuse me?" I couldn't help myself. I wasn't going to just stand there and let the man talk about me like an inanimate object.

"Did you need something?" the aide took a step to insert himself between me and the prince.

"I need to understand why you're talking about me like I'm not close enough to hear you." I rolled my eyes.

"Our discussion isn't about you. It's about the prince and his future. Maybe you would benefit from quelling your ego." again the aide spoke, but Prince Asante held his hand up, quieting the man.

"My ego is just fine. Maybe you would benefit from not assuming women are morons." I scoffed. "I have no interest in whatever it is you think is going to happen here. Choose another woman for the job."

"How could you say you have no interest in the prince?" The aide spoke, and Prince Asante said nothing. "Do you know who you are?"

"Yes, I do. I'm a woman who makes my own choices. And right now, I'm choosing to end this conversation." I looked the prince in the eye. "Find another girl to hang on your arm. Look around, there are plenty who want the chance."

I turned, stomping off, dirt covered and proud of my response. The prince of the fire dragons could kiss my ass!

CHAPTER 2

With a determined stride, I left the prince amidst his fawning supporters, the murmur of their voices fading as I walked away. One glance back found him already swallowed up by the swarm. Everyone wanted a chance to get close to the prince. I hoped he would find someone else to entertain whatever twisted thoughts rolled through his head, or that his aide would convince him to choose one of the other women. But there was something about that look in his eye that told me this would not go away easily.

Once back at my cozy home, I cleaned up the dishes I'd used to start my day and sat on the small chair in the sitting room. Already my body ached, but I knew I wasn't physically tired. It was a mental weight that made my shoulders tighten and my legs throb. The prince was in town and now had his eye on me and, once again, I longed for home. I wanted to be with my people, but I knew I could never return there.

Whenever I missed my true home, I'd open the shuttered windows of my simple cottage and listen to the sweet songs of the lily willows. Delicate little birds with twisted beaks that made their songs sound like the jazz music the ancient humans brought to Lunaterra when they crashed into our world all those years ago. I had never interacted with an actual human or any of their direct descendants, but my father had. And he raved about the beings that so many others wanted to demonize.

It had been five years since I last heard my father's shaky laughter. When something amused him, his entire body became an expression of joy with chaotic jerks and violent shaking. He couldn't help it. He would have outbursts unbefitting someone of his position, but he didn't care. And neither did I. My favorite moments were those spent laughing with my father. My mother complained that I inherited my expressive laughter from him. She tried to train it out of me, but the habit persisted, like a weed refusing to die. At least that's how my mother saw it.

I went to the window, leaned on the sill, and let out a long sigh. The scent of fresh tea hung in the air. When I closed my eyes, the birds almost sounded like her. My mother. I could see her soft eyes and full smile. Yes, she was a mother who wanted the best for her daughter. She was strong-willed, and sometimes pushy, but she was also joyous. She would sing whenever she could. Anytime I found my mother alone, she'd be humming a song and daydreaming about being a performer. I missed everything about her.

It's hard to walk away from everything you know and start over. Especially when you have to do it in secrecy. It's not the way I wanted my life to go, but I saw no other way to live a life I designed for myself. My parents wanted more for me than my *simple* dreams. They actually would have been happy to find out that a prince like Asante had chosen me, even if it was only to appease his mother. They wanted me to be educated, to marry well, to have babies and to live a life where aides helped me do everything.

I wanted a life I could actively participate in. Where I could work long hours doing things I loved. Where I didn't have to hide in corners to sing my melodies. My mother's heart longed to be a singer, to perform in front of crowds. My heart ached every time I had to remember how she gave that all up.

After an hour of thinking about things I couldn't change, I headed out. I couldn't spend the day wallowing. There was work to be done, and customers who depended on me to do it. I pinned my long locs up into stacking buns at the back of my head. Splitting the weight in two meant fewer headaches and a style that would last through long days.

I had to get a head-start because things were a little more difficult for me. Most shop owners in Clayhorn could warm up their equipment with the breath of their dragon. I had to use other means, and I had to do it in secret. I was a woman of ice hiding in a world of fire.

I didn't keep it hidden because anyone would shun me for it. Ice and Fire often intermingled. But I kept the detail to myself because I felt it added another layer of protection. The fewer people who knew, the less likely someone would go digging into my past.

My doors opened just in time for my first customer. That same gray-haired old woman.

"Hello Mesi!" I greeted her cheerfully.

"Happy to see you opened on time." She smiled. "Those other slackers are still trying to get over the shock of our unexpected visitors."

"It's a rare sighting." I shrugged. "I understand it."

"I suppose. Still not sure why he's here." She pursed her lips. "He's barely shown any interest in the women out there. And trust me when I say they are doing everything they can to get his attention."

"Have they not gone yet?" I couldn't help the frown that spread across my face. "That's surprising."

"No, the prince is taking his time. Meeting with the elders of the community. I could have stayed, supposed I should have considered the number of grays on my head, but I have a routine to keep. I need my morning delights."

"Well, I'm happy to be a part of your routine." I smiled.

"You know how addictive your treats are. It reminds me of things I had long ago." she paused, giving me a look that made the hair on the back of my neck stand. "That was a long way from here, though."

"You've mentioned this before, but you never give me any details." I urged her once again to remove the enigmatic veil from her words.

"A girl has to keep a little mystery about herself." She winked at me before shuffling over to the display case where the prepared pastries waited.

After spending more time with Mesi, and bagging up her favorite puff pastries with the yellow flecked icing, I returned to my duties of crafting delicacies that kept customers coming back. They could never understand why they loved my food so much. It was a family secret, one I was so grateful my grandmother had taught me.

My process had a secret ingredient: ice. While folding the dough and mixing the fillings, I infused my desserts with ice, binding it to the molecules. That was the secret. It gave the treats an extra pop that drove the fire dragons crazy. As far as I knew, I was the only person in the land of fire capable of creating these treats.

That day felt different. Tunes I heard my mother sing a thousand times filled my mind. I began humming them as I worked. It started out looking to be a slow day, everyone was still trying to catch sight of the prince. But once the excitement wore off, it was back to business as usual. As the end of the day neared, my shelves were nearly bare.

I whipped up a few more things for the night rush, but felt confident that everything would be gone before I closed up. I was always careful to make just the right number of delights, no leftovers. My creations had to be eaten as fresh as possible, because the crystals I infused them with would melt and disrupt the taste.

I'd just finished arranging the last of the colorful, sweet-smelling treats when the door opened with a chime, announcing a customer. With one of my mother's melodies still in my mind, I turned, humming, to greet my new customer. The smile dropped from my face when I saw who was walking through the door.

In that instance, I heard my mother's voice in the back of my mind saying, *'Child watch your face'.* I'd fought a silent war against my own expressive face my whole life. Whatever feelings I had lurking under the surface would instantly paint themselves across my features. As Asante entered, I was sure my face matched my thoughts. *Please go the hell away.*

His entourage of aides followed close behind. Including the one marked with talons. The old man who looked in constant fear of losing his job. His beady eyes quickly scanned the inside of my shop as the door closed behind their crew.

Asante looked genuinely surprised to see me standing there, as if he didn't know that I was the owner of the shop, so I tucked away my annoyance and greeted him like I would any customer.

"Welcome." I smiled politely. "How can I help you?"

"It's you." A soft smile lifted the corner of his mouth before it disappeared. "Is this your shop? Are you the owner?"

"Yes, owner, baker, and server." I nodded and discounted the fact that it should have been obvious. Perhaps he thought I was just a worker there? "I opened it not too long ago. I'm new to the area."

"Well, we're glad you came." He looked around me at the freshly prepped display case. "I've heard about your desserts all day. The elders even made me promise that I would come here before leaving. You've made quite an impression on this community. Especially the one called Mesi. She was adamant that I do not miss out."

"Word of mouth is the best for business, as they say." Again, I remained as polite as possible while trying to control my expression. I would need to have words with Mesi later. And I don't know what it was about him, but my blood instantly boiled every time he spoke. All I could think about was how he referred to me as 'that one'.

"I received a lot of recommendations about what I should try, but I'd like to know what you think. What's your best dessert here?" the prince asked.

I looked around at the dwindling supply.

"The best thing on the menu sold out earlier in the day. It takes a long time to make, so I won't have more until tomorrow, but," I walked over to the case, opened it and pulled out a small pastry. Delicate layers of dough folded around a soft jellied inside. I placed it on a piece of parchment paper and handed it to him. "Let me know what you think."

I watched carefully as the prince lifted the simple dessert to his lips. A dusting of sugar-coated his fingertips as he bit into the pastry. My smile mirrored his as I saw his lips curve into a joyful expression. Every chef anticipated this moment, the unveiling of their dish, the quiet hush before the explosion of taste and texture. Then came the shift in expression. The slight upturn of their lips, the flutter of their eyelids, the warmth in their cheeks. An expression of pure joy. Confirmation you created something that touched them deeply.

For a moment, the previous arrogance seemed to drain from the prince's face, leaving behind only a look of vulnerability. He didn't look like someone who thought his birthright meant the world owed him whatever he wanted. There was an almost gentle and caring quality about him. A quality that briefly made me lose the desire to punch him in the face.

I was never more patient than when waiting for someone to try my food. Watching the prince, I no longer cared about the people who came in with him. All that mattered was that he savored every morsel.

"I've never had anything like this before." His eyes opened, and he looked at me with something like awe.

"A delicacy taught to me by my grandmother." I nodded and smiled. "This is one of the first things I ever learned to make. So simple, but for a long time, it was my favorite."

"I would love to meet her." He looked around as if my grandmother would appear out of the shadows.

"She isn't here." I shook my head.

"Out shopping?" He bit into the pastry again and smiled. "I don't mind waiting for her to come back."

"No, I mean, I'm alone now. I have no family here." The words were hard to say, but they were true.

"Ah, I'm sorry to hear that." He glanced over at the gray-haired man and nodded. "Domin, I would like to have more of these."

"Of course, sir." Domin nodded and reached for a pouch, which I assumed contained the currency to pay for the prince's order.

"Can you make more?" Asante looked back at me. "How long do you need?"

"That really depends on how many you would like."

"Enough to last me a month." Asante lifted his chin. "I want to have these every day."

"They don't really set well for more than a day. It's why I make them fresh each day."

"I understand. So, if I want more, I have to come back every day?"

"That is impossible." Domin fussed.

The prince paused, a thoughtful frown creasing his brow as he considered his next move. Again, he looked different; his eyes held a newfound intensity, and his posture was more confident.

"I'm sorry if he offended you earlier." His words shocked me as he referred to the man whose name I now knew was Domin.

"It's fine." I shrugged. "You're used to getting what you want. He probably is, too. And all the women out there want you, so you're probably not used to coming across a woman who would deny you."

"I have to ask you. Would you really deny my request?" Asante narrowed his gaze.

"To be your fiancé? Why wouldn't I? You know nothing about me." I scoffed. "Also, I hear how the elders talk about you."

"Oh? How do they talk about me?" He looked amused. "Do I have a terrible reputation?"

"Yes, you do." I said honestly and glanced at Domin, who looked displeased at my answer. "I know it's not right for me to say this to your face, considering your position. But you asked, and I am an honest person."

"Your honesty comes sharp like a blade." He dusted the sugar from his fingertips. "But it's good to know. That's a shame. I suppose I should work to repair that."

"It couldn't hurt." I agreed with him.

"Would it change your mind?" He looked me in the eye. "If I work to fix my reputation, would you be open to my request?"

I considered his question, knowing full well the life he led wasn't one I wanted to be a part of. "No, it wouldn't change my mind."

"You seem sure of that." Asante quickly glanced at the helpers who lined the store before returning his eyes to me. For a moment, it looked like I had embarrassed him.

"I am." I adjusted the apron around my waist. "What you're offering isn't something I want. So, no matter how much you improve yourself or what actions you take to fix your reputation, it won't change that. But I'd be happy to see you repair the thoughts of the old ones."

"Very well." He looked around. "I'll take everything."

"What do you mean?" I asked.

"Everything you have, I'll take it." He waved at the display cases.

"Oh, I can't do that." I refused his offer. "That wouldn't be fair to my other customers. I have regulars who rely on me."

"Interesting." He sighed. "Well, give me what you can. Domin will pay you for everything."

I nodded and turned to bag up the items I could spare, leaving a few of the goods I knew my regulars would come in looking for. Like the buttery breads that Calli came for every night. She loved to have them with her soups. She would hold it against me if she couldn't get at least two of them. I pretended not to hear their hushed whispers and muttered complaints while I focused on my work.

"Why can't you just order her to come with us?" Domin fussed. "If you want her so badly, just make it happen. You're the prince."

"I don't want to make anyone do something they don't want to do. Besides, you know my mother. She will recognize the deception easily. Gather the sweets, pay her, and let's go."

"As you wish."

Asante turned to leave the shop, leaving just Domin and one other woman behind. When I finished bagging the goods, the woman took the bags, Domin paid me, and they left. The second he was out the door, I covered my mouth with my hands and screamed into my palms.

"I hope you never return!" I fussed and stomped back over to the counter.

CHAPTER 3

I desperately wished that would be the end of my interaction with the prince. If I had any favor with the gods, he would fly to another town and find another woman to catch his eye and forget about buying pastries from me. Clearly, the gods didn't give a damn because my prayers for freedom from the royal went unheard.

Two days later, the first order came. And then every other day, a new person arrived with an order for the prince. They would come the night prior, place the order, and then pick it up the next day. Soon that became a standing pick up each morning.

It wasn't long before the pickups included unwanted drop offs. Gifts from the prince. I tried to refuse them, but they would drop them and run like backwards bandits.

And each day the gifts got worse, more elaborate and ornate. Huge baskets overflowing with silks, shimmering jewels, and gold trinkets were unceremoniously dumped onto my counter. To any other woman, it may have been flattering. At another time in my life, I might have felt the same. But every time I heard the convoy's arrival announced by the sounds of dragon wings drowning out the morning birds, I dreaded it. And each time my door opened to find his royal aides carrying baskets of goods, it just made me feel worse.

Some nights, I would go home and contemplate leaving the beautiful life I had cultivated for myself. The prince wouldn't give up, I knew that. The orders would continue along with the gifts and attention that I didn't want from both him and the people I lived around. I wanted peace, and he was taking it away from me.

How long would it be before the gifts turned into more pressing advances?

"You sure you don't want to keep this? It is so beautiful." A woman who visited my shop at least three times a week for berry topped pastries asked as I handed her the basket full of fabrics.

This had become a part of my closing routine, ending my day giving away the wares that came from the prince. The scent of their jealousy hung heavy in the air as I pretended not to notice their envious glares and the sharp whispers that followed them out, their arms full of treasures they could normally only dream of owning. They benefited from my nuisance, but they wanted it for themselves. And if given the opportunity, I was sure they would push me off a cliff to take my place.

"Of course I am, besides it makes your eyes pop so well!" I stretched a fake smile across my face as I lifted a piece of fabric to her cheek. "And your complexion just screams to be wrapped in this fabric."

"You know, I think you're right. Thank you!" She grabbed the fabric from my hand, stuffed it back into the straw basket she carried on her shoulder, and ran for the door. They always ran away as if they were stealing something, afraid that I would change my mind and tell them to give me back the things they took. Some of them even purchased more treats, I guess as a way of easing their own guilt about taking the things that weren't meant for them.

After weeks of this routine, I had all but given up hope it would ever end. And on a night when a chill had set in. I was closing up my shop when the bell called my attention to the front as the door opened one final time.

"Sorry I'm closing." I turned around with a warm smile, expecting a late customer who would take whatever scraps they could get. "There isn't much left, but take whatever you need."

"Perfect timing then." Standing in front of me wasn't a random customer or even an aide from the court. Asante. I suppose he had given up on having other people come and do the running for him.

"What are you doing here?" Was it the appropriate way to address the prince? Maybe not. But I was shocked that he was in front of me.

"Did you not like the gifts? You've given them all away." He pretended to be hurt, but I could tell by his expression that he didn't care about the superficial items he had sent my way.

"Not really my style, honestly." I admitted. "Bushels of flour and fruit would have been better for me, considering what I do here. The jewels and the fabrics were nice, but I don't really get a lot of time to play dress up."

"I suppose that would have been a more thoughtful gift, considering how much I've been purchasing from you." His lips tightened with a nod. "I'll keep that in mind."

"Is there anything I can help you with??" I looked around him, expecting to see his guards. "Did you come here alone??"

"Yes. As a matter of fact, I did come here alone. I didn't want anyone here with me when I talked to you. You see, I have been scratching my head, trying to figure out what it is about you I can't stop thinking about. And in the time since I saw you. I've enjoyed your sweets. And I have realized that's what it is. It's the things you make with your hands, the way your food makes me feel. So, I wanted to come here to see you without distraction."

"Without distraction?" I swallowed the lump in my throat. "Your team would be a distraction to you."

"I have a proposal." He nodded slowly.

"I'm not interested in marriage." All I could think about was getting ahead of him. Stopping him from asking me something we would both regret.

"Not a proposal of marriage. You rejected me once and I won't have that happen again. A business proposal."

"A business proposal? What kind of business could we possibly have together?"

"I want you to come with me," he hesitated. "I'd like for you to work for me."

"You have plenty of people working for you." I laughed at the idea. "What could I possibly do that they cannot?"

"These delicacies that you have. I've tried to have them recreated. None of my cooks have been able to figure out what you do to make them so delicious. Just as you said before, in time, they always taste worse. Even the time it takes for them to fly them from here to me, they lose something. Something magical. And I think the only way I can address that is to just have you come work for me. Cook where I eat."

"Oh." Despite the shocked look on my face, I wasn't at all surprised to learn that they had failed.

"I know this is a shock. And it may be hard to walk away from what you built here. But I will pay you well for it." He looked around my shop as if considering the gravity of what he was asking and yet still he proceeded, "Will you do it?"

"No." The last thing I wanted to do was sign up to be locked away in a palace making treats for a prince. That was even worse than the thought of being forced into a marriage with one.

"No?" His jaw tightened once again. He didn't expect me to reject him. The hurt in his eyes told me he believed my rejection was simply a manifestation of my unwillingness to commit to marriage. Even without the promise of love symbolized by a cold, hard ring, a new name, or a sense of nobility, I felt content with my life. Why would I give that up?

In an instant, as quick as a lightning strike, his demeanor changed. That softness that caught my attention earlier hardened. Ridges appeared around his face, as if he was holding back a shift from his dragon. This was not a prince accustomed to being told no.

"You would continue to reject me after all I've done?" He spoke through a tightened jaw. "How could you be so ungrateful?"

"Did I ask you to do anything for me? You sent your gifts and purchased your sweets, and you expect me to do what exactly? I don't want to walk away from everything I have here and come live there and cook for one person. I do this because I enjoy seeing the faces of people who enjoy my food."

"I am more important than these people," Asante boasted.

"Says who?" I shook my head and stepped away from him, disgusted. "What about you wanting to change your reputation here?"

"I have a lot on my plate. For weeks I have been sending money into this town, buying your treats. And respecting your decision to decline my first proposal. I know who I am and if they can't see that even after all that, it's not up to me to fix."

"And maybe that's your problem." I hoped no one would hear what he said. "You think you're better than the people here simply because of your status. A status you did not earn but were born with. You are no better than they are."

"I withdraw my proposal." Asante scowled at me. "This is no longer a request. I'm issuing a demand. You have seven nights. Wrap things up here and come to the Crown. And if you don't, I will send someone for you."

"Excuse me?" I backed further away from his dark expression. "You can't be serious right now."

"I'm not one for telling jokes."

I had to swallow back the urge to reveal the secret I had kept for so long, one that could get me out of the unwanted position. But it was a secret for a reason. Instead, I swallowed back the words. I'd have to find another way out of this mess.

"This is a good thing for you." He reached around me and grabbed the last puffed pastry from the counter. "You'll earn more and be safer."

"Are you just going to ignore me?" I laughed. "You expect me to believe this is about my safety now? I told you I don't want to go."

"I heard you. But this time, I'm the one rejecting what you want." Asante turned and left the shop. The little bell above the door ringing as it slammed shut.

CHAPTER 4

Seven nights to get my affairs in order. And just like he said, on that seventh night, they arrived. Employed to the crown, workers who shut my shop down, packed my things from my home, and carried me away. And I let them. It made no sense to fight them.

I didn't want to make a big scene in my small town. Stories of the prince kidnapping a woman would travel far and wide. If it did, the wrong person might hear it and come to investigate. So, I said my uneasy goodbyes to those I'd become accustomed to and left it all behind. Mesi came to clean out everything she could before they ushered me away. Once again, there was something in the way she looked at me that made me feel unsettled, but I filed it away with all the things that no longer mattered.

I sat uncomfortably in the seat atop the dragon carrying me from my peaceful home to the center of Starwell. Before I climbed into the carrier on its back, I said a quick apology to the dragon and hoped it would forgive me. Even so, I wished they hadn't made me ride. Minutes into the flight, I realized I'd seen very little of the side of the island claimed by the fire dragons.

When I ran from my home, I wasn't much interested in sightseeing, but in the hope of choice. And because I wanted to stay hidden, I'd never allowed my wings to carry me across the land. It was too risky. So, I'd gone without shifting, which meant no flights and minimum traveling. Although I was being carried away against my will, I was able to appreciate what felt like a new world to me.

Starwell was a mirrored version of Frostspire. Full of flush valleys, mountains, rivers, and fertile earth. Birds followed our path, separating and rejoining as they rode the current the larger beasts created. I closed my eyes and savored the ride. I imagined diving off the side of the dragon, unleashing my own wings, and joining the birds.

Just a few hours after leaving, we landed in the center of the royal grounds. And everywhere around us there were preparations happening. It took a moment for me to remember, but this was the time of the festival. Joyous occasions when people came together from all corners of the world. In addition to the festival, there was also a wedding approaching. The rumors of it had spread quickly through Clayhorn. A royal wedding that might reshape the political landscapes. If I had been back home in Saldann, I would have been an expected part of the celebrations. And odd things since the dragons never attended the actual celebration. Still, we loved a party, so we would simply do our own thing in Saldann. I guess the fire dragons felt the same way.

It would be exhausting and overwhelming and my mother would constantly fret about my hair, my skin, and my outfits for the weekend. Not anymore. It didn't matter. What did matter was surviving whatever the hell the prince had in mind for me.

"You're here." The annoying voice of a little man with too much power at his disposal reached my ear.

"It's not as if I had a choice." I turned to find Domin standing with a smug look on his face.

"Indeed." He sighed, almost rolling his eyes at me. "The prince was adamant about you coming to work here, so I guess I should welcome you."

When he said nothing else, I shrugged and looked around the open courtyard. "Am I just supposed to stand here or is there something for me to do?"

"Uradis will take you to your room." He pointed at a tall, dark-skinned woman with soft eyes and long brown hair who appeared beside him. "You will remain there until further word."

"Thanks." I said simply and turned to the woman.

"Follow me." She spoke with a deep voice that made me imagine a powerful dragon living inside of her.

"I'm Kiala, it's nice to me you…"

"Uradis." She nodded tightly only glancing back over her shoulder for a moment.

"Uradis, that's a pretty name." I tried to make small talk, hoping the woman was softer than she appeared.

She smiled. "Thank you."

We headed inside the palace, which was a blend of gothic and modern touches, the result of meshing generational shifts in taste. Some parts of the palace were dark, untouched, and covered in cobwebs. Yet others were bright, open, and full of greenery. It reminded me of my own home. Passed down through our family for so long that every person left their own unique touches.

As much as I hated to admit it, the prince's home was beautiful. I could feel the love that someone had poured into every carving, every structure, every pillar we passed. But then there was this other air of sadness. An invisible blanket that covered the halls, the furniture and the people I saw passing by, and I knew what it was.

This place and these people were mourning.

Uradis spoke as she led me to my quarters, but I became distracted by the murmurs around us. They talked about the prince as if he was a mythical creature. I chewed my lip as a short woman referred to a prince who refused his duties and made his mother, the Queen, upset. The loudest voices came from ahead of us as we neared the doors to the room Uradis said belonged to me.

"I just don't understand how he could do this right now. There's only one thing she wants from him, and all he wants to do is sit out there and train those dragons for a competition they won't win," the voice of an older woman spoke.

"Well, the convergence games are important to him. You know that it's what his brother would have wanted," another younger voice whispered.

"Are you saying his brother's wants are more important than his mother's?" The woman sounded personally offended by the concept.

"I don't think either one is," the younger voice defended. "I think what matters is what he wants. But again, I wasn't born of royalty, so choices like that are up to me to make."

"I guess it is a double-edged sword, isn't it?" the older woman spoke as we stopped outside the door.

Uradis looked at me and winked, letting the conversation continue. Her willingness to do so secretly pleased me. I wanted to know what the women truly thought.

"Indeed, it is." The younger woman sounded like someone ready to end their day but forced to do more work. I was sure the old woman's fussing made it worse for her.

"And now this woman from Clayhorn is coming." The older woman continued to complain, now referring to me. "We're meant to prepare for her. We have no idea who she is, but she's taking up one of the best spots in the place."

"Maybe the Queen will get what she wants after all."

"I doubt it." The older voice scoffed. "From what I've heard, this woman doesn't even want to be here. She's the one who makes those delicious treats. But since our chefs haven't been able to replicate them, she's supposed to be here to do it herself."

"He complains of not having the ability to choose for himself. And now he's doing the same to her." The younger voice scoffed.

"While that may be a valid sentiment, it's best you not let anyone else hear you speak on it." The older voice gave the stern warning.

Uradis had heard enough of the conversation and chose that moment to push the cracked door open. The tired, rusted hinges sang their woes and announced our arrival. She cleared her voice and eyed the women who held onto their whispered conversation. The woman with gray hair and green eyes nearly jumped out of her skin and dropped the folded blankets she carried.

The younger woman covered her mouth with her hand, trying to hold back laughter. She was embarrassed but had clearly been careful in the way she spoke in case someone overheard them. The older woman was not as smart.

"I thought this chore was done already," Uradis addressed them.

"Oh, yes." The older woman nodded. "We're done, just adding some final touches. I'm sorry. We'll go now."

"Gossiping wenches," Uradis muttered after the two left the room.

"Excuse me?" I acted shocked to hear her say that, but after she let me overhear what they were saying, how could I be? I stepped quietly into the room and glanced around at my new "home".

"My apologies. I just hate to hear people talking about things they know nothing about. They should be smart enough to understand how complicated all of this is. For the queen, the prince, and now for you. It's easy to stand aside and make such judgments when your life isn't being upturned."

"It's okay." I looked around the room before turning back to her. "You know they're not all that wrong, anyway. At least about me."

"You didn't volunteer to be here?" She chuckled. "You mean to tell me this wasn't your dream?"

"No, not at all." I shrugged. "But what the prince wants, the prince gets, right?"

"I'm sorry to hear that, but I must admit that the way you get under Domin's skin gives me such joy." She winked. "He is a pain. He takes his job far too seriously. It's as if he thinks something or someone will kick him out of the picture."

"Is that what it is?" I pursed my lips. "That honestly makes sense when I think about how he responds to me. He's overprotective of his position."

I thought Domin was just a jerk. But maybe he was a jerk who was afraid of losing his job. A prince finding a bride could do that. Often when royals married, there were staff changes to accommodate the couples' new needs.

"I used to think he was just being overprotective. Just trying to make sure his role was secure. But now I'm not so sure. All I do know is he gets on my nerves and seeing someone get under his skin the way you do, makes me so very happy. So, thank you."

"Well, I'm glad to know something good has come from all this."

"I'll let you get settled in. The others will bring your things in a few moments. We like to let the Stagnants rest before unloading. They're a lot less agitated that way. Let me know if there's anything you need."

"Thank you. I appreciate that."

Uradis walked out of the room, leaving the door slightly ajar. Because I didn't want anyone peaking in on me, I headed over to close it. Then I heard it, whispers of a passing pair of men. I held the door as still as possible, hoping they would pass quickly. I wondered if every court had this many gossips.

"The trolls have made another approach."

"Do you think she will let him go?"

"After losing his brother like that, I doubt it. The queen wants the prince to focus on what's important."

"A wife and child." The shorter guy scoffed. "Prince Asante wants no wife and child. The sooner his mother accepts it, the better. He enjoys coaching those dragons for the games. Maybe she should let him get it out of his system."

"She will never accept his refusal to continue their bloodline. Who would rule if that happened?"

I waited until I could no longer hear them before finally closing the door. And once again, the hinges sang like birds in the morning as I pushed it closed.

With my back to the door, I sighed. "What the hell did I get myself into?"

The knock on the door startled me. It must have been the aides dropping off my items. I straightened and opened the door. But it wasn't the women I'd left my items with. It was the prince.

"You're here." He smiled as if I would be happy to see him.

"As if I had a choice in the matter." I rolled my eyes and stepped back from the door to let him enter the room. "Come in."

"You did have a choice." He stepped inside. "But you chose wrong."

"According to you."

"I need you here. It's important to me." He looked around the room. "I even gave you one of the best spots in the place."

"There are plenty of people here who can make you those sweets." I lied. "And I liked my own home a lot better than this."

"I don't want anyone else to make them. I want you to make them. Must you be so difficult? I pulled you out of there, wasting away. Now you can live here."

"Trapped in these gray walls instead of free to roam in nature like I love? Oh yeah, you've done me a great favor here."

Asante frowned at me. "You do know who you're talking to, right?"

"Yeah, I do." I tapped my chin with my finger. "The prince running from his responsibilities to play coach."

"Who are you to talk about my responsibilities?"

"I'm no one. That is what your people say." I reported part of what I heard rumored in the hall, leaving out the troll attack.

"My people." He narrowed his eyes. "What people have you heard say that?"

"Oh, I don't know their names. I just got here." It would be foolish to tell him about the passing men. He might find out who they were and then retaliate against them. And that might stop people from gossiping, and I needed the intel if I was going to figure out how to get away.

"Well, forget what you heard." He ordered as another knock sounded on the door.

This time it was the aides with my things. The prince excused himself as they brought in my items. As soon as they were done, they left me alone. I spent the rest of the day organizing my things and trying to think of a way out. The idea I came up with was to just walk out the door. Why make things complicated when they didn't have to be?

There was no security detail. After my dinner had been served, a meaty stew that was too hot for the season, they left me alone entirely. So, after peeking out my door several times and finding no one monitoring me, I grabbed the few items I cared about, stuffed them into a woven bag, and tossed it over my shoulder. With my face hooded by the cloak I threw on, I was off to make my escape.

I thought I remembered the path Uradis took as she led me through the massive halls, but apparently, I was too busy eavesdropping on the passing gossip. After several wrong turns, I landed exactly where I didn't want to be. I stood outside a cracked door. The smell of food came from within, the same hot stew I'd eaten earlier. And with the delicious smell came the sounds of two people arguing.

"Don't you dare stand there and disrespect me like this!" one woman spoke in hushed anger.

"Disrespect you? How am I doing that?" I recognized Asante's voice instantly.

I held my breath and tiptoed closer to the door.

"Lower your tone." She fussed. "You're ignoring what matters."

"This *is* what matters to me, mother!"

My heart ached as his voice cracked.

The pain I heard.

It was the same way I felt. Trapped in a family who thought they knew what was best for me. Every life choice felt predetermined; a path laid out before I even understood I had a say. It was the reason I left home.

A beat of silence, the weight of the prince's frustration heavy on me, derailed my escape route.

I jumped when I heard footsteps moving down the hall toward me. I stumbled backward, hoping to find a place to hide, but bumped right into a guard. He narrowed his gaze at me, glanced at the cracked door, and shook his head. Then, against my will, he ushered me right back to my room.

CHAPTER 5

I wish I could say the angry queen and her tantrum-throwing prince kept me up all night. That their images swirling in my mind somehow prevented me from drifting off to sleep. Or that the sounds of their imagined shouting echoing in my ears. But that would be a lie.

I slept like a baby.

That bed had to be the most comfortable thing I had ever laid on before! I'd heard about the warming beds the royals had, but this was far more amazing than even the rumors made them out to be. The moment I laid down in that artificial cocoon, everything that worried me melted away. I could have stayed in that bed for many days, lost in the soft comfort of the down. But the sun's sharp light through my window and the cacophony of battle—a symphony of screams and clashing metal—forced me to wake.

That's when I realized that my new bedroom, the one *he* assigned me to, overlooked the training grounds. And so, as I stumbled from the bed over to the window, I found prince Asante, with all the men he was set to train. These are the men that would take off and be a part of the convergence games. The tournaments that determined who were the best our world had to offer.

As I watched him, I understood why he wanted to train the others. The sheer mastery of his skills evident in every precise movement made the time he spent guiding them worthwhile.

Asante himself moved with the grace of a dragon's current, a swirling dance of power and fluidity. Every action he showcased, as his sword danced more like an extension of himself than as a weapon he held, felt purposeful.

A knock at my door interrupted my viewing.

"Hello, Kiala, it's nice to meet you." A cheerful woman with bold makeup and a bright smile walked into the room after I opened the door. "My name is Maryl, and I am to help you while you get yourself adjusted here. You're going to be working in the kitchen with myself and the rest of the cooks. I understand you are here to make special treats for our prince. No one gave us a list of accommodations for you, but if something is missing, just ask me and I'll make sure you get whatever you need."

"Oh, thank you." I smiled as if I really wanted to be there. "It's so kind of you."

"They also told me you don't exactly want to be here," she said, and the smile fell from my face. "So, I won't treat you like the others. They're already planning to isolate you."

"I'm sorry, what?" I gawked at her blatant honesty.

"Don't take offense, but we have some of the best chefs and dessert pastry cookers around the world working here. Not everyone here is a dragon, so for you to be brought here to create something that none of them could master, it's kind of a big deal."

"Ah." I nodded. Of course, no one wanted to be made to look incompetent at their job.

"But if you really wanted to leave, perhaps you could share your secrets?" she looked hopeful.

"Thank you." Even if I wanted to share my secrets, it would make no difference because none of them could replicate the process.

"Here is your uniform." She handed me a bundle of fabrics. "This is only to be worn while you're in the kitchen. When you're out of the kitchen, you can wear whatever you want, but our queen does visit the kitchen from time to time and we must be presentable when she does."

"Right. Thank you." I took the bundle from her and started looking over the soft gray and red fabrics. At least the material was soft. It wouldn't irritate my skin.

"I'll give you some time to get ready. I have to go check in with some other people, but then I'll be back to escort you to the kitchen."

"Thanks, again."

Maryl left me alone and I got myself together, fixed my hair and put on the soft fabrics. I couldn't help but roll my eyes at how horribly boring the outfit was. The gray blended into the background and the touches of red represented fire. That was it. Of course, it didn't matter how I looked. I was going to stand in the kitchen and get messy. No one was going to be looking at me.

Moments after I finished dressing, Maryl returned to get me. I followed her through the busy halls to the kitchen on the lower level, where I immediately got to work. Their eyes followed my every move. It didn't feel safe even pretending to do the treats the way I'd normally would. So instead, I made them how everyone else would. Simple ingredients put together in a bowl, baked and prepared the best that I could without using my magic.

The idea that my treats would end up less tasty just because I couldn't steal a few moments to myself disheartened me. But after a while, I smiled to myself, thinking this could be my way out. Maybe if they didn't taste as good, he would send me away from his home and back to my shop. Maybe I could convince the prince that I had to be happy and comfortable to make them to the best of my ability.

It was a long shot, but it was worth a try.

When I finished making the treats, Maryl came and got me to usher me to the prince.

If he hadn't taken my freedom away, I might have found him attractive. Sitting beneath a stone arch covered in red and white flowers. The prince stood and greeted Maryl and I as we approached him.

"Maryl, it's good to see you again."

Maryl said nothing. Her face brightened as she smiled, bowed, and waved her hand at me to present me to him.

I stood there, tray in hand, and Maryl ran away. It was like she didn't want him to even look at her. Her chubby cheeks flushed crimson, and a little giggle escaped her lips. Something told me Maryl had a crush on the prince. I immediately concocted a story in my mind about Maryl one day stealing the heart of the cruddy prince. And as I've told myself this story, Prince Asante stood looking at me like I was an alien.

"Are you going to present the treats to me?" He asked, a frown etching itself onto his face, clearly annoyed.

"Oh yeah, sorry. Here you go." I pushed the tray out to him.

"You look a mess." He turned up his nose as he looked me over. I was covered in flour and had a little dried egg still on my hands.

"Thank you so much for the compliment." I huffed. "I only spent hours slaving away in a hot stove in a hot, unfamiliar kitchen that is not my own, struggling to make the most basic desserts, because your kitchen doesn't have everything that I need."

"Sorry." He said shortly before peering over the presented treats. They looked good enough, but I knew they wouldn't taste the same.

I watched him as he ate the food and awaited his reaction. I knew it wouldn't be the same typically when someone ate my food. Their eyes lit up and their face is flushed, and they looked like they were in heaven. That is not what happened when Asante put those morsels into his mouth. His brow furrowed; his nose scrunched up. He looked at me with total disappointment.

"Did you purposely make them this bad?" He dropped the uneaten food back on the tray. "They don't taste anything like what you gave me before."

"I don't purposely destroy food, but your kitchen is not the same as my own place. The tools are not the same. And I don't like being watched when I do what I need to do. The reason other people can't do what I do is because they don't know my secrets. And you want me to sit there and do everything with an audience. I walked into the kitchen and their eyes followed me everywhere. How could I work like that?"

The prince looked away from me. "Why didn't you mention this before?"

"I feel like this is something I'm going to be asking you a lot, but when did you ask?"

"What do you need to make them better?"

"Why are you spending so much time training those men?" I avoided the question and redirected the conversation to something I was more interested in.

He frowned at me. "What are you talking about?"

"You know my room overlooks the yards." I rolled my eyes as if he didn't know. "I assume you had me put there on purpose. You wanted me to see what you were doing with your days. Am I wrong?"

"I didn't select your room. My aide did." He lied straight to my face. "I'm training those men because they have to go to the tournament. Because I want them to win and bring honor to our people."

I could have pointed out how he'd already told me he chose my room, but I kept the thought to myself. "Isn't there someone else who can do that? Does it have to be the prince?"

"The person meant to do it is no longer here with us. I'm filling his shoes the best I can. And I'll tell you, like everyone else who asks, no, I don't think there is anyone else." He took a deep breath, his jaw tightening with aggravation. "This is personal to me. I need to do this. Is that a good enough answer for you?"

"I didn't intend to offend you." I pulled back on my prodding. "I just wanted to understand why it was so important. I've only been in your home for a day and already I've heard so many rumors about how you are refusing your responsibilities and your role as a prince to focus on this. And so, yeah, I'm curious as to why this was important."

"This will be the first time in a long time our people are able to take part." His shoulders relaxed. "It was supposed to be this grand return to the world. You're a dragon, you understand how this works. How long has it been since either us, the fire or the ice dragons, has even stepped foot off this island? Finally, we have been making strides to return to society. This is one of those last steps when we go out there and we show them what we're made of." Prince Asante turned to look out at the open sky and a gentle breeze picked up as he continued. "We need to make a strong showing if we want to get back into the world. It's infuriating to think of the drama that kept us locked away for so long, and now we're finally at the precipice of getting back out there and I can't let all that hard work go to waste. So yeah, I am putting a lot of my time and attention into this. When I'm done, I will return my attention to my other *princely* duties. I just wish people could understand that."

"I never really understand why we withdrew from the world, either. We shied away when things got tough, and I don't get it." Two sides of the same coin, fighting for years until that fight spilled out into the rest of the world. That was until both sides decided to retreat to the island and keep to themselves.

"It's because in this world, if one of us cannot be out, neither can. Anytime the fire dragons stepped out, the ice dragons would cause havoc. And the other way around, too. We don't want to be seen, but we don't want the other person to have the spotlight either. It's pathetic, and it's time we change that. I only wish I could somehow contact the leaders of Frostspire. It would be good if we both took this step together, but that is beyond my position right now, so I'm focusing on what I can and I'm hoping I can lead by example."

"Have you ever explained that to anyone like you have to me? They would understand it. Maybe they wouldn't question you so much."

"It is not my hope to get understanding from simple-minded people. They're only focused on considering the status quo. I must push outside of that and don't get me wrong, I've tried to explain this. Until I had no breath left in my lungs I tried, and I still went unheard. So now I can only focus on what I can do. Let my actions and their results show them, not my words."

"I can appreciate that sentiment." And there it was. Sympathy. Here I thought he was just arrogant and used to getting his own way, throwing a tantrum when someone refused his requests. Yet really, he and I had led similar lives. None of this was what he actually wanted, either. We wanted to break out and do something unexpected, but our families had already decided what we should do. If I hadn't run away, I'd be just like him. Under the pressure of expectations from people who didn't understand me.

"It's not your appreciation I am after. But I'm going to ask you again, what do you need to make these better? Because honestly, these have been the only thing to bring me even a small bit of joy lately. It has been hard and I'm searching for whatever good I can get."

I paused for a beat, wondering if there was a way to convince him to send me home. The longer I looked into his eyes, the less I believed that was possible. Even in those moments of sweetness with him, there was still an edge, still something underneath the surface, some part of him that was still a prince. A prince who believed he deserved everything he wanted, no matter how it affected other people. He was a man who had been told his entire life that the world owed him a favor. And so instead of asking for my freedom, I asked for a bargain.

"Give me a place where I can create in private." I spoke. "I don't want eyes on me while I do what I need to do."

He eyed the tray in my hand and nodded. "I will have that arranged."

"Thank you." I turned to leave, but stopped when he spoke again.

"I heard you were out for a walk last night." Prince Asante gagged me with his words. "You must have gotten lost because you had to be escorted back to your room? Are you alright?"

"Yes, I am. New place and all." I waited for him to mention the bags I had with me, wondering how I could explain them.

"It can take a while to adjust." He smiled.

"Yes." A nervous smile stretched my lips as I returned his, silently praying I hadn't been exposed.

"Kiala, next time you want to go for a stroll, leave the luggage behind." He moved toward me, his expression almost threatening.

His eyes glanced up over my head at the door behind me.

I heard the rhythmic footsteps of women reverberating in through the empty hall behind me. Before I could turn away to see who was coming, a wave of female voices — sharp, high-pitched, and overlapping — surrounded me, drowning out my own thoughts. Asante's arms wrapped around my waist, pulling me close as his lips found mine.

"Asante!" a woman shouted.

He released me, and I turned, my face a mask of confusion, to see the queen standing there. The way she looked at me — eyes blazing, fists clenched — made it crystal clear she wanted to punch me.

CHAPTER 6

"What is this?" The queen's voice was like daggers in my eardrums.

"Mother!" he acted embarrassed, but I knew if his act didn't fool me, it surely wouldn't fool his mother. He grabbed my hand and held it down near my hip.

"Explain this." The queen pointed at me. "How could you be out here kissing the help?"

The *help*? If not for the thought that this would get me out of my unwanted arrangement with the prince and back home to Clayhorn, I might have said something.

"This," he paused and turned to smile at me. "This is the reason I don't want to entertain your proposals."

"What?" the queen echoed the question in my head.

What the hell was he talking about?

"I've found someone who brings me joy." Asante's smile beamed across his face. *Very convincing.*

The queen looked me up and down. I could see the disgust on her face. I did not measure up in her opinion. I stood there, a low-level chef in my flour-dusted uniform, the smell of baking bread filling the air. Her disapproval pierced deeper than any argument with my mother had ever done.

I pulled my hand away from Asante as his mother stepped closer.

"We need to talk about this." She scrunched her nose as she glanced at me. "Alone."

Taking the not-so-subtle hint, I bowed and ran the hell out of there. As I dashed back to my room. I was sure this was it. The queen would issue an order for the aides to send me away!

Asante had tried to change the game, but his mother still ran the court.

I made it back to my room, cleaned up, and changed into my travel clothing. I'd twisted my long, thick locs, which now reached nearly my waist, into a neat bun and pinned them at the crown of my head when a knock came on the door. The sound echoed through the quiet room.

"It's me." Asante's voice, quieter and less confident than before, called in to me.

"Come in," I answered, ready to be told the Queen wanted me gone.

When he walked into the room, the joy for my anticipated freedom dissipated and a renewed anger replaced it. Once the door was closed behind him, I marched over to him and slapped him right across the cheek. The sound echoed around us as he grabbed his cheek and cursed under his breath.

"Have you lost your mind?" He looked at me, his own rage in his eyes.

"Never kiss me without my permission." It was all I could do not to hit him again. "I don't care who you are or what crown you wear on your head. I'm not a toy to be used when you want to upset your mother."

"You're right. I was out of line." He nodded. "I'm sorry."

"Why would you do that?" I huffed. "Why would you put me in that position?"

"I saw an opportunity to shut my mother up, and I took it." His callous words did little to calm my nerves.

"Shut her up? You think this is going to shut her up?" I stepped away from him. "How does making me look bad shut her up?"

"In hindsight, probably not." He adjusted his collar. "You saw how she is. Pushy, overbearing."

"I can't say from what I just saw that I would classify her as anything but a mother shocked to see her son kissing—a stranger. Besides, even if that is the case, do you think that means you can just have your way with anyone?"

"I apologized and yet you're still going on with it."

"You call that an apology? You know what, you're right. I shouldn't continue with the topic. Instead, I'm going to pack my things and leave."

"What?" He grabbed my arm when I turned from him. My eyes dropped to the point of unapproved contact, and he let me go.

"I'm not staying here, and you can't force me to." I boasted.

"Technically," He started, surely about to throw his weight as prince in my face.

"Technically, maybe. But do you want to explain to your mother why you're forcing the woman you kissed so freely to stay here?" I challenged him. "Do you think I won't make a fuss for everyone to hear? I'm sure it will make it back to her. Just like my walk made it back to you."

"What exactly do you have that's so good to go back to?" he asked. "I can provide everything you need here."

"Let's see, my *life...freedom!*" I threw my hands up. "I would think *you* would understand that?"

The prince took a deep breath and pinched the bridge of his nose. I watched him as he considered how to continue the conversation. What could he possibly say to convince me not to leave?

When he looked back at me, his eyes pleaded for my empathy again. "Please, just stay long enough for the games to be over. Once that is done, I'll deal with my mother. But as long as you're here, I think she will stay off my case. If you could just pretend to love me, I will let you go as soon as this is done."

"You want me to pretend to love you?"

"Yes, it's called acting. You've heard of it, right?" he smirked. "I'll even make sure you get all the time you want to roam in the fields like you seem to love to do. As long as you make your treats for me. The real ones, not those things you served me today."

"How long?" I contemplated his offer. Maybe there was a way I could get something out of this arrangement for myself.

"What?"

"How long will it take?

"The tournament is in a month." He nodded. "After it is done, this will be over."

I left him waiting as I weighed his request against what I needed for myself. What could I ask for as a bargain for staying? Simply going back to living in obscurity didn't seem like enough. I needed more than that.

"There has to be something you want." He offered before I could even form the words to ask. "Whatever it takes to make this work, I'll make it happen."

"I want to leave." My heart ached a bit, but that was what I truly needed. An escape.

"What?" he scoffed. "I mean, yes. I will send you home."

"I don't mean back to my home." I corrected him. "That's not good enough. I need to leave Saldann for good. Can you help me do that?"

"Why?" I frowned. "What are you running from?"

"That isn't your concern." I scrunched my nose at him. "That is the condition for me to stay here and help you fool your mother."

He stared into my eyes, looking for some glimmer that my stare would betray my secrecy before agreeing. "Okay, yes. I can help you. Where would you want to go?"

"Aghon." I thought of the land of the orcs. It would be the best place for me. Far enough away from Saldann that no one would think to look for me there. It would also allow me room to let my dragon free.

"You want to live with the orcs?" He frowned in judgement of my choice.

"Is that a problem? Why does it matter to you where I live?"

"Fine. I can make that happen." He agreed. "That's a fair exchange."

"Promise it." I squinted at him and pointed to his chest. "A real promise."

"Is my word alone not good enough?"

"After what you just pulled?" I crossed my arms. "No. It isn't good enough."

"Fine," he sighed. He lifted his finger, and it shifted to dragon claw. He then opened his shirt and dragged the nail across his chest. "I promise to uphold my end of this bargain. I will personally escort you away from Saldann to the land of the Orcs when our deal is done, where I will leave you to live free and in peace. As you wish."

I couldn't believe he'd actually done the dragon's promise. This was *binding*.

If he didn't keep up his end of the deal, his lie would form into a poison. One that would wrap around and strangle his heart until he died. I peered into Asante's eyes, the silence heavy between us as I waited for some betraying tremor. Some subtle shift to reveal his true intentions.

A sharp, loud rap on the door shattered our eye contact, making us both jump.

"Come in." Asante called out and when the door opened, the pest entered.

Domin, the annoying man who clearly hated me, eyed the fresh scar on the prince's chest.

"Sir, there is something that requires your attention." He glanced at me, then back to the prince. "Queen Toci requests your presence."

"What is it?" Asante asked.

Domin looked at me again, a slight tremor in his hands betraying his reluctance to speak before me.

"You can say it. It's fine."

"An injury with one of the trainees." He paused. "And a problem with the trolls at the borders."

"They're here again?"

"Yes." He nodded. "Their boats touched ground last night. The scouts reported it not too long ago."

"I'll be right there." Asante stared at Domin until he left the room and then turned to me. "So we have a deal. We'll talk about this more when I return. Stay here until someone comes to let you know it's safe."

"What's going on with the trolls?" I had heard nothing about trolls visiting Saldann. If they were showing up unannounced, it wasn't a good thing.

"It's nothing, just political nonsense. Don't worry about it." He closed his shirt and adjusted his collar. "Stay here, please."

Each minute after he left stretched into an eternity. I kept waiting to hear a voice assuring me of safety, but none came. Finally, I looked out my window and saw the prince, his shoulders slumped in solitude on the training grounds. The late afternoon sun painted the scene in hues of orange and gold. Maybe he had forgotten about me. But it certainly didn't look like there was trouble approaching.

Bored with my room, I decided this was the best opportunity to show him I could keep up appearances. If this was going to work, I would have to be seen with him. It had to look as if I cared. A sullen prince needed to be comforted. Who better to do that than his pretend love interest?

I left my room, dressed in a flowery gown that told a story of budding love with each step I took. With some effort, and directions from a passing woman carrying armfuls of silk, I found my way to the grounds where he stood sword in hand and pained expression on his face.

"What are you doing?" I asked as I approached. "You've been out here by yourself for quite some time now."

"Working through my thoughts." He looked up at me and, for a moment, smiled. "Domin was right, one of our men was hurt. He fell off a cliff and broke his arm and leg. He won't be able to fight or shift for a long while."

"I hope he heals quickly. Are you able to replace him?"

"No, not really. We just have to hope the healers can fix this. I'm not confident it will be in time for the tournament."

"Do you plan to stay here until they do?" I pointed at the empty grounds around us. "Will you sit here in protest?"

"No." He chuckled. "But I'm not sure what else to do with myself now."

"Well, I'm supposed to be your love interest here." I tapped my chin with my finger. "I guess I should come up with something to take your mind off things, right?"

"Really leaning into the role, huh?"

"I do nothing half-assed." I lifted my chin. "A loving woman is supposed to care for her man. That's what I'm here to do."

"What do you have in mind?" He straightened then spoke with a teasing tone. "Oh loving woman of mine."

"Nature." I didn't let his dropped smile deter my enthusiasm. "We need to get to nature. It is healing and provides clarity. Can we do that?"

"Nature?" He looked around at the grass. "This isn't enough?"

"No, I mean *real nature*. With animals, trees, bugs, and dirt. All of it, not this carefully manicured lawn." I corrected his thinking. "Extra points if there is a waterfall nearby. It's how I center myself."

"Alright, we can do that." He grabbed my hand. "Let's go."

Asante led me to the stables where the serabringers were. These creatures were the product of the stagnant dragons that had interbred with an equine species that once lived on our island. Serabringers combined reptilian scales, powerful equine legs, and a long, serpentine neck. The quadrupedal creatures possessed medium-sized wings, which aided their running speed, though they were far too small for flight. The beating of their wings made a whirring sound as they ran.

Their creation was one of those things shifter dragons didn't talk about much. While Serabringers were a part of our bloodline, we chose to ignore the actions that led to their existence.

I loved Serabringers and missed the ones we had in Frostspire. The only difference was the color of their hair. In Frostspire, they had a blend of white and brown hair, which often grew longer to brush against the ground as they walked. But here in Starwell, serabringers had bright red hair and strong features.

"They're all so beautiful." I smiled as he pulled two of the creatures from their stalls.

"I used to love hanging out in here with them. Until I grew too old for such games."

"You're never too old." I took the reins of the smaller one, who nuzzled my jaw with her nose.

"Tell that to my mother." Asante smirked and helped me onto her back.

"What's her name?" I patted the enormous head in front of me.

"This is Synth," he told me before also introducing his. "And this is Kune. Kune was my brother's."

"I'm sure they're both ready to ride." I smiled.

After an hour, we found ourselves in a picturesque, wooded area, thanks to Synth and Kune. We secured the serabringers to a sturdy oak post before setting off on our hike through the dense, fragrant forest. The scene was beautiful: meticulously carved paths worn by previous visitors snaked through the landscape. With each step we took, I felt my soul heal. This trip might have been to help him, but it was doing wonders for me.

As we walked, Asante talked about his family. His father who was away on royal duties, his mother who buried herself in meaningless tasks to avoid her mourning, and his brother who had recently passed away.

"What happened to him?"

"Trolls happened." Asante focused on Kune as he spoke. "He went out there hoping to broker peace. The reports that came back were inconsistent. Some said the trolls attacked, others claimed it was an accident caused by a storm. That they never even encountered trolls. So, because of the inconsistencies, we can't take any direct action. Especially since he wasn't supposed to be there. Tarak took the trip against my father's wishes, and it cost him his life."

Asante took careful steps away from me as he continued. "I believe it was an attack. The state of his body, that wasn't simply because of a storm. The healers even ruled it out. They said all evidence pointed to an assault. But because of how the reports came in, my father chose not to take action. And every day I think that was a mistake."

"And now the trolls are here again?"

"They were, but they've turned back. Peace continues. At least for now." The silence stretched between us until Asante turned the questions on me. "What about your family? Where are they?"

"I don't know." I told the lie I had been perfecting for years.

"You're out here all alone. With no one to watch out for you?"

"A lot of people are alone, Asante," I said. "Some of us choose to be that way."

"Why would you choose to be alone?"

"It doesn't matter."

"I have been honest with you." He stopped walking. "Why are you hiding so much from me?"

"You don't need to know that much about me. I won't be here long, remember?" I circled him and then began my climb up the small, grassy slope, and inhaled the scent of pine needles that filled the air. Though I tried to appear confident, his question had thrown me off and it suddenly occurred to me I had no way of escaping him. Distracted by my thoughts, I missed the danger ahead of me. After only a few steps, my foot twisted into the decaying vine and I tripped. The sudden impact jarred my ankle as I fell. The yelp, a sharp, involuntary sound, escaped my lips as I stumbled backward.

As I braced for impact, a wave of mortification washed over me. This would be the second time I fell on my ass in front of the prince. But I never hit the ground.

Asante was right there, cradling me in his arms.

I looked up at him. His dark eyes felt less intimidating. There was something else there, something I saw the first time I met him. It betrayed the hardened edge the prince held onto. It was soft, vulnerable, and it made my stomach flutter.

"You can keep your secrets," he whispered. "One day you will trust me enough to tell me."

"I-," I started, but he cut me off.

"Please don't slap me for this."

Asante leaned in and kissed me again.

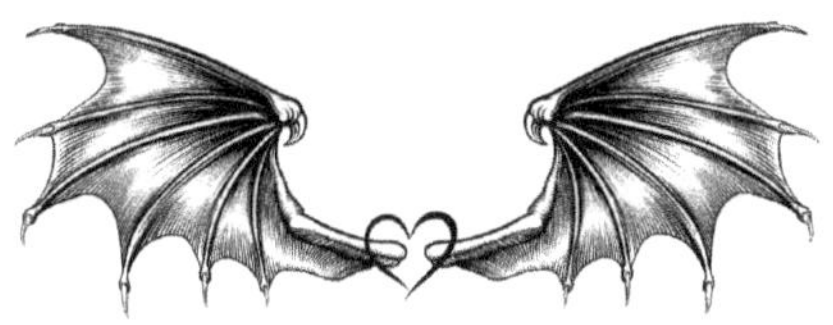

CHAPTER 7

The kiss lasted longer than it should have. But with his lips pressed against mine, I felt something deep within me respond. A long-dormant part of my soul suddenly awakened, surprising me with its intensity and power. It felt like a hidden wellspring bursting forth. I tried to suppress it, shove it back into hiding. And for a moment, I felt like I might actually win that battle. Then his arms tightened around me and his hand gripped the back of my head.

Everything about him overwhelmed me. The deep scent that rose from his flesh, the warmth of his hold, and the sweet layers of his kiss. I gripped his shoulder, pulling him deeper into the kiss. When the soft moan slipped from his lips, it shocked me back into the moment. What we were doing was wrong! I couldn't let it continue. I snapped out of the temporary trance his lips had put me in and pulled away from him.

Unfortunately, the kiss also made me forget about the pain in my ankle.

When I pushed him away, he simply let go without a struggle. And I fell backward, this time hitting the ground with a thud. My ass banged against the unforgiving earth and a jolt of pain shot up my spine. It felt like fire as a stinging erupted in my ankle, spreading rapidly up my leg with a burning intensity.

"Ouch," I cried out and pulled my leg to my chest to ease the discomfort, but it didn't help. "Damn that hurts."

Asante kneeled beside me. His hand hovered over my ankle, clearly afraid to touch it and make it worse. "Are you okay?"

"I must have really gotten it twisted in those vines." I narrowed my gaze at the cluster laying on the ground as if they had purposely attacked me.

"Can you stand on your own, or do you need help?"

"I should be able to manage." I tried to get up but the moment I put any weight on the leg, I almost fell back over and he had to catch me, again, to keep me from hitting the ground.

"Aren't you glad we came out here to be with all this *real nature*?" he joked.

"Very funny."

"We need to go back now." He looked at my ankle. "Do you think you can shift? We'll fly back and I can send someone to get the serabringers?"

"No!" I blurted my objection out so brazenly that he looked at me like I had lost my mind. I hurried to make an excuse for my outburst. "I don't think shifting would be a good idea for me right now. The pain is a lot more intense now, which probably means it's a more serious injury. Shifting could make it worse." I was a better liar than I thought.

I paused, waiting for him to consider my excuse. His expression shifted back from surprise and confusion to concern.

"You're right, you might have broken something." He looked around us. "That shift could mean putting you down for a while. I'll have to carry you."

I thought he meant carrying me in his dragon form, which could be dangerous in my condition, but that's not what he meant. Without another word, he scooped me up from the ground, careful not to lift my dress. Once he held me to his chest, he looked down at me.

"Is this okay?"

I wrapped my arm around his neck for more support and nodded. The only thought swirling in my mind as he carried me back to the serabringers was how ridiculous I looked. I have never been a damsel in distress, but that's what I looked like. Right down to wearing a nice flowery dress to complement the moment. This was the stuff small girls were told to look forward to and it made me sick to my stomach.

And of course, the longer he held me, the more I felt the warmth of his body. And the more the kiss replayed in my mind. How would that moment, that lapse in judgement, change things between us? I should have slapped him. I should have cursed him out. But even in that moment of fleeting regret, I didn't want to.

"Don't worry. I won't tell anyone about this." His voice was as strong and unfaltering as ever.

"Oh?"

"That's what you're worried about, isn't it?" He glanced at me. "I will keep this kiss to myself. No one will know you allowed it."

"Is that supposed to be funny?"

The lift at the corner of his full lips lasted for just a second, but I saw it. "No, of course not."

"It's not right for you to make fun of me when I'm injured and can't get away from you."

"What do you mean? That's the best time to do it."

"I'll remember this."

"Sure, but what will you do about it?"

The subtle sound of neighing brought my attention to the serabringers. They were nuzzled together under the tree where we left them.

"Enough of that," he fussed at them as if they could understand him. I smiled because it reminded me of all the times my father would do the same thing. "It's time to go."

"Okay, put me down."

"What do you mean?" He tightened his hold.

"How else am I supposed to ride?"

Asante looked like he wanted to laugh in my face. "You can't ride like this. I'll have to carry you."

"What?"

"And risk you falling off?" He walked me over to Kune, who folded his wings to allow Asante to put me on his back. After I was secure, he tied Synth's rein to Kune's before hopping on his back with me.

"Are you comfortable?"

"Yes." I looked back at him.

"Good." He wrapped one arm around my stomach, pulling my back into his chest as he kicked Kune into gear. The two creatures ran forward in unison.

I couldn't help it. A part of me melted into him as we moved. The warmth of his fire reached through the sheer fabric of my dress and made my entire body flush.

"Hold on," Asante whispered in my ear before he urged them to move faster.

As my luck would have it, we arrived at the stables in front of a crowd of people. They watched as he carefully climbed down and untied the connected reins. Synth ran back to her stable, no guidance necessary. He then turned back and held his arms out to me.

"Let's go."

I hesitated, but the pain still throbbed in my leg. He was right. I wouldn't have been able to ride alone. I thought of protesting for a moment, but then I realized that complaining would probably just prolong this unintended performance in front of the crowd. So I conceded and allowed him to carry me from Kune's back.

"Prince Asante!" Domin ran over to us. "Are you alright?"

"I'm fine," Asante stated, a hint of annoyance coloring his voice as he looked at the bewildered man and then nodded curtly in my direction. "She is the one who is injured. Let's get her to the healers."

Domin didn't care about me, but he feigned interest, anyway. "What happened to her?"

"She fell. It should be a simple fix for them." Asante answered.

"I'll get this taken care of," Domin said and gestured to a guard to come help.

"I have her," Asante said with an air of protective warning.

"As you wish." Domin responded through gritted teeth. "I'll go ahead to get them prepared."

He turned and ran off ahead of us.

"He really doesn't like me." I chuckled as Asante carried me.

"He just wants me to be okay. Everyone here does."

"I supposed that is good. You know I'm not here to hurt you, right?"

"How could you be? I forced you to come here, remember?"

"Oh, yeah. Right." It was strange that I wanted to defend myself. Something inside of me wanted Asante to know that I wasn't whatever Domin thought I was. But he was right. It wasn't my idea to be there, so why would anyone suspect I had ulterior motives?

"Did you forget that I have you here against your will?" his brow raised.

"Of course not!" I fussed.

"Sure," he paused. "It's almost like you've changed your mind. Like you want to be here now."

"Don't flatter yourself." I rolled my eyes. "Be quiet. All this talking is making my ankle hurt more."

We arrived at the healers, and Asante handed me over. They were eager to take me in and fussed about the way he held me.

"Your grip is far too tight." A short man patted Asante's arm. "I've always told you that."

"I'm sorry, Uncle Eivek." Asante smiled as he lowered me to the bed. "Please take good care of her."

"Oh, so this is the one." A tall, slender woman with bright eyes said. "We'll give her our very best."

"Thank you," he said, and we shared an awkward glance.

The one.

Hearing those words spoken aloud sent a shiver down my spine; it felt strange and unsettling.

"What happened?" Asante's uncle asked.

"She fell," Asante began his explanation, but was hushed almost immediately by a hand in front of his mouth.

"It's your leg that hurts, correct?" Eivek asked. "So, your mouth works just fine?"

"Yes," I answered.

"Great, tell me what's wrong. And don't let this one start talking for you. Trust me, he will never stop. He's just like his father in that way."

"Must you treat me like a child?" Asante huffed.

"Yes, because in my eyes, you'll always be one." He patted Asante's arm again before turning to me. "So tell me everything."

I went into detail about the vines that wrapped around my ankle and caused me to fall. I left out the part about the kiss, choosing instead to cut to the point in the story when I landed on my ass.

"I think I might have hurt my tailbone as well."

"We'll make sure we're thorough in checking out your injuries." He grabbed a small stone cup from the tall woman and handed it to me. "Drink this. It will stop the pain and might make you sleep while we work. It is the ideal condition. The more relaxed you are, the more effective our practices are."

I looked at Asante for reassurance. When he nodded, I took the cup and drank the warm liquid. It had a powerful spiciness that was only mellowed but the strong earthy taste. I swallowed the liquid hard. Before I could make any comment on the taste, my body went limp.

"Well, that worked faster than usual! Usually takes a bit for it to contend with your inner fire. You must be in a lot of pain if your flame is that weak."

Part of me was glad to hear him say that, as if it validated all the attention I was receiving. Then I turned to Asante, whose face grew wearier with his uncle's comment. The flash of concern that this was a bad idea was too late. There I was, slipping into unconsciousness, an ice dragon in the land of fire. What could possibly go wrong?

When I woke up, Asante was gone, and in his place was Uradis.

"You're awake." She looked down at me with a mothering expression. "How do you feel?"

"Groggy." I looked down at my ankle and rolled it a bit to see if there was pain. It still hurt, but not nearly as much as before. "That's amazing. There's barely anything at all."

"The Royal Healers," Uradis said proudly. "They have some extra tricks up their sleeve."

"I'm glad." I scanned the room once more, acknowledging the disappointment that Asante wasn't there with me. "Where is he?"

"The prince?" She smiled knowingly. "He had some business to take care of. So he told me to stay by your side. But now that you're awake, I can take you back to your room and make sure you're comfortable. We also need to get something for you to eat."

"You don't have to do all that for me." The last thing I wanted was to have someone fuss over me. "I'm sure I can manage on my own."

"You might be okay with turning down Prince Asante's requests, but I am not." She raised a brow. "Besides, you're the prince's intended. Of course I do."

"So, everyone knows about that now?"

"That his mother caught him kissing you and he proclaimed you were the one to bring him so much joy? Yes, word spreads quickly." She chuckled. "Besides, the prince carrying you across the field to the healers gave everyone quite the show. If they didn't know before, they're definitely speculating about the relationship between you two now. Some of them are even whispering that that's the only reason you're in the position you are in now."

"Great," I muttered.

"Let's test your strength." She stepped away from the bed to give me room. "Please stand. Take your time. We don't want to cause reinjury."

I stood, but my legs gave way a little, and before I could steady myself, her hand appeared with a cane.

"Use this for now. You shouldn't need it for long."

"Thank you."

"Ah, she is awake." Eivek entered. "Uradis, do you mind if I have a moment alone to discuss prognosis?"

"Of course. Take your time." Uradis left the room.

There was a part of me that wanted to scream for her to stay. What did he know? I gripped the cane and stared at him, hoping my face was hiding my anxiety.

"It looks like you're going to be just fine. Actually, I'm glad to see how well you're doing with your injuries. I was expecting it to take a lot longer for you to heal, but there's something special about you, isn't there?" He gave me a look that reminded me of Mesi. There was a cold, knowing glint in his eye.

"What do you mean?"

"I'm a lot older than the one who helped me take care of you. So she might not see the difference in you, but I do." His brow raised. "Ice to my fire."

"I-,"

He put his finger to his lip to stop my impending rambling. "There are moments when secrets need to be revealed. This is not one of them. I'm going to accept that this is one thing I don't need to know all the facts about. But be careful. I am not the only one here who can discern these things."

I tightened my grip around the handle of the cane. "Thank you."

"Does he know?" Uncle asked.

I shook my head.

"Promise me you'll tell him before his heart gets too deep into this. Asante presents an image of hardness, but you've gotten close to him. I can tell by the way you two look at each other. You can see that beyond that tough exterior, he's a gentle person, one who gives his heart fully to whatever he cares about. And he cares about you. I've seen him hurt a lot, and I don't want you to add to that."

"It won't come to that."

"Good. Now. Uradis is waiting for you. It's best not to make her wait too long. Rest, eat plenty, and take care of yourself."

I looked at the door. "You're not going to tell?"

"I'm old, but I'm not without my ways. I heard the circumstances of how you came here. I also know about the promise mark on his chest. Whatever is between you must stay that way. Asante believes you need to be here, enough to carve a promise across his lifeline to make it happen. And if this is what he thinks he needs right now, I will not take that away from him. All I ask is that you bring him peace and not heartache."

"I won't be here long enough to do that."

"So, you don't intend to marry him?" He smirked. "Is it all just a farce?"

"He has a plan." I chose honesty.

"This makes so much more sense now." He sighed. "Looks like my nephew got around his mother's pestering ways. Even better. Finish your bargain and leave him whole."

"I will."

I left the room to find Uradis standing down the hall from the door. I wondered if she had overheard any of our conversation. Her warm smile when she saw me didn't seem like one of deception. With a brief nod, I joined her, and she led me back to my room.

Along the way, it seemed everyone was staring at me, and I could see what she meant. Some of them looked at me with awe, others looked at me with pity, and still others looked at me with hatred.

And I understand that look.

I didn't belong. I was an outsider. Someone who came from a background unfitting that other princess. And I was in a position that some would even have killed for.

It was jealousy. Jealousy for something that they didn't know they wanted. Something that they could never have. Something that I didn't want at all.

Uradis and I made it back to my room, and I watched her as she made sure that everything was in place. Shortly after we got inside, there was a knock at the door, and I had to internally pinch myself for hoping it would be him.

It wasn't the prince on the other side of the door. It was a woman with a tray of food. Uradis let her in so she could put the tray down and quickly ushered her away.

"Where did he have to go?"

"I'm sorry?"

"I know I shouldn't ask this, but it's been on my mind since you told me he had to run away. Is it something to do with the trolls?"

"And where did you hear about the trolls?"

"The walls have ears and mouths," I said.

"Yes, well, they're back. We thought they had gone, but once again, they landed on our shores. I just wish we knew what they wanted. You know how they like to conquer new places. It's like a sport to them."

My heart dropped into my stomach at the thought of a war with the trolls. "They want to take over?"

"Yes, and they know our people are split, so it'll make it a lot easier for them to do so."

"What do you mean, split?"

"I mean the ice dragons."

I hadn't heard anyone refer to my people as belonging with the fire side.

"If we were a united front, it would make it a lot harder for the trolls to just come over here and run us over. We're split. Our forces halved, solely because we don't want to work with each other. But better we cooperate with each other than be run out by others, right?"

All I could do was nod. To lead her down further conversation about the two dragon species would be to betray her in a way I didn't want to. I wondered if she was the only one who thought of fire and ice as being one and the same. I stared down at the bowl and acted as if I was starving.

"That smells fantastic."

"The best our kitchen offers." She gave another cursory glance around the room. "Eat up and rest well. Maryl Will be back in the morning to take you to your new kitchen."

"New kitchen?" I gasped. "There's a new kitchen?"

"Yes, special requests by the prince. If the cooks didn't hate you before, they surely will now. Should be a fun day tomorrow!" She laughed as she walked out of the door.

CHAPTER 8

I devoured the food because I was hungrier than I thought. And it really was as good as I said. Just like everything I'd eaten there, it had a spark of fire that warmed me to a state of total comfort. After bathing and hobbling back to the bed, I quickly fell asleep.

The next day, as in previous mornings, Maryl met me at the door. I expected her usual bubbly demeanor, but there was something off about her. Her smile wasn't as bright. It didn't take long for me to realize it was because of Asante. When I first met her, she seemed pleased that I didn't want to be there. It was like a relief for her. But with rumors spreading about our supposed engagement, she could no longer feel the same.

"You must be happy to have your own space." Maryl said as she opened the door to the private kitchen. "I know it must have been so uncomfortable for you yesterday, what being with the rest of us low cooks and all."

My heart thumped at her sudden harsh attitude toward me. "Yes, thank you. It's only because I'm not used to working while being watched."

"Of course." She didn't even try to hide her disbelief. "No one has needed to be in here since they built the larger kitchen. But we worked all night to clean it up and make sure it was ready for you."

"I really appreciate that. Thank you."

"Let me know if you need anything." She gave me a tight nod.

"I will. Thank you."

"Oh, and you won't have the wear the uniform anymore. Since you're not in the main kitchen, the queen won't care what you wear. She never comes in here. She's always hated this space. Said it was too small and smelled funny."

I wrinkled my nose at the thought, but found relief that I wouldn't have to worry about any uncomfortable meetings with the queen. "Okay, thank you for letting me know."

I thought about asking her about Asante. The strained, almost painful, curve of her lips stopped me in my tracks. So instead, I thanked her once again for helping me. And she left me alone.

This kitchen felt more like my bakery. Quiet, small, and much cozier than the large, overpopulated space where the others worked. I didn't feel like I was in the way or being monitored.

I looked around, inspecting the equipment and making sure everything I needed was there. He'd even stocked it with my preferred ingredients.

My mind raced back to the thing I wanted to forget. The kiss. My face flushed with heat as I thought about how he caught me from my fall. And how he asked me not to hit him. I should have slapped him if for nothing but to keep the distance in our relationship. The problem was, I didn't want to. The more I thought about it, the moment we shared, the way he cared for me after I was hurt, even his uncle's words, the more I realized something was changing between us.

"Get over it, Kiala. The kiss wasn't that good." I told myself before I got to work. Eventually, he would come, and I wanted his desserts to be ready for him.

But something was different. I hummed, a soft melody that I only sang when I was my happiest. I paused. Hands deep in the dough I was kneading. My stomach fluttered and my pulse quickened. *Did I actually want to cook for him? Was I happy about feeding him?*

"This is going too far!" I slapped the dough. "I'm only here until the deal is done! Then I can live the life I truly want. This is not the life I want!"

I spent the next few hours making the best versions of my desserts that I could. With my privacy, I could do the process exactly how I would any other time. There was no one to watch me pull the ice. No one to report me to the queen for doing the practice.

How would they feel about having an ice dragon cooking for the prince? Maybe they would think someone sent me there to hurt him. Would they capture me? Punish me? A wave of anxieties washed over me as these thoughts raced through my mind. And what would Asante think if he ever found out who I was? What would it mean for him if anyone else did? But my worries didn't stop me from doing what I needed to do. And by the time Maryl returned to take me to him, everything was ready.

As before, she led me straight to the prince. Only this time, there wasn't any chatter. No talk about what the other workers said or did. She walked me there, had an awkward exchange with him, and then left us alone. He was in the same spot as before, underneath the flowered arch.

"You're all right." I said once we were alone.

"Shouldn't I be asking that about you?" He looked down at my ankle.

"I'm fine." I lifted my ankle and rolled it around. "It doesn't hurt at all anymore. I didn't even need my cane."

"That was fast." He frowned. "Are you sure?"

"Apparently, I wasn't as hurt as I thought." The lie left a funny taste in my mouth that I ignored.

"Well, that's good. And why are you worried about me being alright?"

"You weren't there when I woke up." I admitted. "I expected you to be."

The corner of his lips lifted; he liked that I wanted him there. "I'm sorry, I had to take care of something."

"Is everything alright?"

"It is, and it will be even better if those desserts taste like they did the first time I had them." He pointed to the tray in my hand.

"Have at it." I pushed the tray towards him and watched him to pick a dessert.

He pondered for a moment before choosing the jelly filled roll dusted with essence of fire flower. He peered at me, his brow furrowed, as if worried I hadn't done them right. The silence hung heavy in the air.

"They're good. Just try it." I urged him.

"I trust you." He closed his eyes and bit down into the pastry. And a moment later, his expression shifted into one of pleasure, his eyelids fluttered, and he moaned softly. "Mmm. Finally."

"How are they?"

"They're perfect." He took another bite. "Even better than before, if that's possible."

"Good." I sat the tray down on the table next to him. "I'll leave these here with you. I need to go get cleaned up."

"Put on something nice." He said, after picking up another pastry. "I like the dress you wore yesterday. Do you have something else like that?"

"Why?" My brow lifted in suspicion.

"I would like to take you to dinner." He admitted.

I laughed and crossed my arms over my chest. "You want to have dinner with me? Like a date?"

"We are supposed to be keeping up appearances, right?" he looked at me. "How would it look if we shared no time together apart from you delivering these creations to me?"

As he moved closer, his breath brushed my cheek, and my pulse quickened with anticipation. "I would treat the woman I intended to marry much better than that."

"Of course." That was the only thing I could think to say that wouldn't betray me and reveal the response I had to him. As he came closer, a feeling of anticipation, like butterflies, took flight in my stomach. Afraid to find out what would happen if we remained close, I stepped back and awkwardly turned to leave. My face flushed with heat when I heard his chuckle behind me. He was proud of himself.

Hours later, a quiet guard escorted me from my room. When the knock sounded on my door, I found relief to open it and see no one I recognized. I had feared he would send Domin. I didn't care if Asante or anyone else believed me. I knew my gut instinct told the truth. That man didn't like me, and I didn't like him either.

I fussed over my dress, a soft lilac color with red detailing throughout the skirt. That was the one thing I missed about my old life, the dresses. As much as I wanted my freedom, I hated that it meant giving them up. But I couldn't realistically parade around my bakery in lacey gowns that were too expensive for my income to cover. It would have raised my customers' suspicions.

I thought we might be going somewhere away from the palace. Somewhere we could get privacy, but apparently Asante meant what he said about keeping up appearances. Because the guard led me to the picnic style dinner setting in the center of the massive garden that sat east of the palace. Underneath a canopy of bright yellow and purple leaves, Asante stood waiting for me. He smiled at me, completely ignoring the salute the guard gave him before leaving us alone.

"This is beautiful," I commented as the leaves rustled gently above his head.

"Well, I know you like nature, but I didn't want to risk taking you out far again, just in case."

"I told you. My ankle is fine."

"I know, but my uncle gave clear instructions to keep you off of it as much as possible. You're supposed to be resting. Not going on nature hikes. And besides, but my uncle is not one to be disobeyed."

"The two of you are very close, aren't you?"

"Yes, we are. The curse of being the second born. Important, but not the focal point. I spent a lot of time with my uncle while my parents prepared my older brother for his duties as future king." He paused. "My uncle was there for me when it felt like everyone had forgotten me."

"And what about now?" I asked. "Now that everyone is looking at you?"

"He is still there." Asante nodded. "He helps me stay grounded. I expected none of this. I was content to live my life as the brother of the king. It felt like the best option. I see what my father has gone through. Missing out on so many things because of his duties, but my uncle was always there."

"I thought he was your mother's brother." I let the words slip before I could think better of it. Shouldn't I know their family history? Royalty or not, if I were a fire dragon, I would know those things. Asante didn't seem to think it was a problem.

"Many people think that." Asante smiled. "It's understandable. He refers to her as sister because they've known each other for so long, but he is my father's brother."

"I'll have to thank him for taking such care of me."

"He'll say your resting and healing is thanks enough." He ushered me to the padded seating on the ground. "Is this comfortable for you?"

"Yes, it is. Thank you." I adjusted the dress around my legs. "So, tell me, what else should I know about you?"

"Excuse me?" He asked as he began plating our food from the basket.

"I'm supposed to be your love interest, I should know more about you. At least the basics."

"You're right. If anyone asks, you'll need to be able to answer honestly."

"Exactly. So, lay it on me. Tell me everything important about Prince Asante."

Between eating and drinking, he told me everything about him, from his childhood into his adulthood. He told me about his brother and how he felt his mother wanted a daughter. Asante boasted about how proud he was of his father and how he wished he could spend more time with him. Our conversation moved between serious topics and lighthearted ones.

It was during a bout of laughter when a voice interrupted our pleasant meal.

"Isn't this nice?" The queen spoke, standing across from us in the garden. Neither of us had heard her approach, her footsteps muffled by the grass covered grounds.

"Mother." Asante stood and I followed suit. "What are you doing here?"

"Am I not allowed in my garden?" She looked around him at me. "I see you two are enjoying it here."

"Yes, we are." He moved closer to her and said something under his breath I couldn't hear.

"If only she was from a good bloodline." The queen said, and I heard that just fine.

"Please, just leave."

"Fine." She paused. "But I want time with this woman. Kiala. I hope you'll join me for tea tomorrow."

"Of course," I bowed. "It would be an honor to have tea with you."

"I'm sure." She turned her nose up, shot Asante a hard side glance, then left.

"You don't have to do that." Asante returned to me. "It's not necessary."

"Of course I do. If this is going to look legit, I must appear to care about what your mother thinks of me."

"She will try to find out everything about you. I know she already has people investigating you."

"I would expect nothing less. You are the prince, after all."

He laid a hand on my arm, his eyes intense and unwavering as he spoke. "Are you sure you're okay with this?"

"Of course." I pulled away from his touch. "I'll keep my end of the bargain, you keep yours."

CHAPTER 9

We spent the rest of our dinner talking about the queen. It was hard to shift the topic away from her.

"It's not that I don't love her. I adore my mother." Asante finally admitted his true frustration with the queen. "It's just hard to accept feeling like an afterthought my entire life and now, suddenly, because my brother is no longer here, I'm the priority."

I didn't comment on anything he said. I let him vent, and when he was done, he escorted me back to my room.

Despite the frustrations of the evening, something else happened. As we spoke, I noticed a shift in my response to Asante.

How my eyes lingered on his lips when he spoke and how my heart fluttered when he smiled. Though I told myself not to allow it, there was a new fondness there. Even more than that.

As I bathed, cleansing the stickiness of the night from my skin, my mind repeated those sweet moments I couldn't forget. Our hands brushing against each other when we both reached for the bread. When he wiped the wine from my chin with the napkin when I laughed mid-sip and spilled a little. Each of these brief encounters during our time together collided in my mind. Even moments before that night. When he made his promise to me.

I climbed into bed, trying to clear my mind of these thoughts, but couldn't. And as I tried to force myself to sleep, his face and smile appeared before me. His full lips, powerful jaw, and broad chest. I couldn't help myself. As I pictured him, wiping my chin with the napkin and licking his lips after tasting my desserts, my hand slipped between my thighs. I squeezed my eyes shut as I continued playing those moments in my mind, holding on to them as my fingers danced across my clit.

In my mind, I pictured Asante, his hand replacing mine as he hung above me. Each stroke of my finger was his own. Replaced once by his tongue and then by something more. I arched my back as I imagined him kissing me and clinched the sheets as I neared the moment of sweet relief.

"Mmm," I moaned, biting my lip as the breeze from the open window brushed across my chest. "Yes."

I kept going, allowing myself this release for the first time in too long, with visions of someone I claimed not to want in my mind. And when I finished, sweat once again on my skin, I smiled at the moon outside my window. At least I could walk away with something to inspire me on nights when I needed that release. Asante could be that for me, if nothing else.

Instead of Maryl knocking on my door the next morning, a trio of women greeted me. They had armfuls of fabric and makeup, ready to dress me for tea with the Queen. There would be no kitchen duty for me that morning, no treats to take to Asante. As they ushered me to the vanity to start their work, I pushed away my disappointment. Would I even see him that day? Why did it matter to me?

I considered asking if I could make my own treats for the Queen. That thought went out the window when I realized there was a chance she would recognize them. It wouldn't have been unlikely for her to have visited with the Ice Dragons in her position, and if she had, they would have served her their best dishes, including similar treats to mine.

So instead of asking for additional accommodations, I allowed these three women to take their time prepping me for the meeting. They pinned my hair up into a tight bun. Making ringlets with my locs that framed my face. If it wasn't for it being so tight that my eyes felt like they were going to pop out of my head, I would have loved the style.

After finishing my hair and makeup, a light airy look with, they made me stand. I filled my lungs with my last breath before two women held me in place. The third then wrapped a light green corset around my waist. The accessory was a torture device that would make it impossible to breathe. How was I supposed to eat in that thing?

Instead of complaining, I endured. It was one tea, one day. I had to do my part. Make the queen like me enough to get her off Asante's back. If I could do that, then I would have held up my end of the promise.

"You look lovely, dear." The matron of the group spoke as she secured the final ties of the corset.

"Thank you." I choked out.

"Just remember, he's her baby, her only baby now, so she's going to be a lot more protective of him," she continued talking absentmindedly. "Had you come a while ago, before his brother passed, this wouldn't be so hard."

"Yeah, they weren't banking on him being the one to continue the bloodline," the young woman with short blonde hair spoke. "But now it's on him. So, things are going to be a lot tougher for you here."

"Hard to imagine having to start over now," the matron continued. "His brother was already set to be wed soon. And she was such a sweet girl."

"I'll keep that in mind." It didn't matter to me who Assante ended up with or if his mother really thought I was worthy of continuing their bloodline. My womb wouldn't be a part of the equation. I only had to keep up the show for a little while longer. "Is there anything else I should know about her? Anything she likes?"

"Hmm, our queen loves humor, but when it is proper. She likes patience and someone who listens." The advice sounded more like a warning.

"Right." I nodded. All I heard was to keep my jokes to myself and don't rush her. Good enough.

"Don't let these two old ladies get you all upset about this." The woman I assumed was the youngest spoke. "It's going to be fine. If Asante likes you, I'm sure the Queen will as well. Like they said, she's just overly protective right now, and she wants to make sure he ends up with someone good for him."

"I hope I can be that." I nodded. "Thank you for the reassurance."

"I'm sure you will do just fine." She grabbed my hand. "Now it's time to see the queen."

They took me to the room where the queen sat. It was the same room that I stood outside and heard her arguing with Asante the first night I got to the fire dragon's home. I wasn't sure what I expected walking through the door. Maybe something opulent and over the top. Tall and imposing statues looming over me, suffocating. I'd been in rooms designed that way before. Royals often used things like that to make their guests feel smaller.

But it was a simple setup in the center of a large room. Tall pillars, swathed in vibrant orange vines emitting a sweet, intoxicating perfume that saturated the room, lined the walls.

At the center of the room was a round table fixed with a simple tea setup. On the table were sweet pastries, colorful fruits, salty crackers, and creamy cheeses, accompanied by two sets of fine teacups. I walked to the table and stood by the chair meant for me and waited. A few moments later, the Queen entered. A group of women, whom I had seen with her at our first meeting, surrounded her. They didn't join us, they only stood by the door as the Queen walked over to me.

Queen Toci was more beautiful than I'd stopped to give credit for before. She had a presence that made the world stop and give attention. Her skin was a rich umber and glistened with the protective oil she used to coat herself, an effort to protect the dragon within. Though she was far my senior, she still held a youthful presence. Despite that, she was still as intimidating as any queen I'd ever seen.

"I'm glad you could join me."

"Of course, I wouldn't have missed it." I did a small curtsy.

"Please," she gave me a gentle smile that betrayed the way I thought she felt about me. "Sit."

"Thank you." I returned her smile and sat just a moment after she did.

Before we started our conversation, the server filled our cups with tea and took the glass tops off the deserts that covered the table. When she was done, she rejoined the others along the wall by the door.

"How did you meet my son?" The queen got right to the point. No need for extended pleasantries. We both knew why we were there.

"He visited the town where I lived and came into my bakery after some of the locals recommended it," I explained between bites. "He enjoyed my sweets so much that he often sent his aides to acquire more for him."

"So, you moved him with your food?" She chuckled. "Just like his father."

"I'm sorry?" I lifted a brow.

"The King. When we first courted, I would often feed him sweets that my mother made. I'm not like you. I don't have the skill myself." She sipped her tea. "But he loved them so much that he didn't leave me alone."

"Well, now I see where he gets it from." I grinned.

"I've had my people look into you and they weren't able to find much at all. They visited the small town you're from. And, from what I understand, you simply appeared a few years ago." She narrowed her gaze at me. "No explanation as to your home or your family, even the people there know little about you. Why is that?"

"It's true, I keep to myself, but that's not a mistake. It's by design." I straightened and told my truth. "I don't want to be a part of everyone else's world. When I moved to the area, I hoped to cultivate a quiet, peaceful life. An existence that was small, quiet, and undramatic."

She laughed. "Then here comes my Asante."

"Exactly. I wanted peace and freedom. I didn't go there looking for love or to catch the eye of a prince. But one day, a prince walked into my bakery, tasted my treats, and fell in love with them. When he requested I continue making them for him, I did not know it would lead to this."

"Why do you want to be with my son now?" she asked. "If it wasn't your intention before, what has changed?"

"You might expect me to have some story about wanting to lead this territory by his side and be the best for these people, but that's not the truth. While that sounds heroic, my presence here is not a selfless act. My life before Asante was good. But I wasn't completely happy. Asante swept me away from that with a promise to give me the life I truly want for myself. He made me feel like I could have everything I desired. It is very selfish, and I understand if that is not the person who you want to be with your son. My choice is one for me." Everything I said was honest, if a little edited.

"I can appreciate a person who knows what they want for themselves. Even more so, I can appreciate that you didn't completely uproot yourself solely at Asante's request. You chose this path for yourself. I commend you for that." The slight twitch at the corner of her lips hinted that the queen was doing a little editing of her own thoughts.

"Thank you for understanding." I nodded but, if she appreciated it, why was she so scrutinizing of me?

"And what about your family?" She pointed to my tea, and I took a sip. "I understand you wanted to be alone, but you have to understand my position here as the Queen. If I am to allow this to move forward, allow you to be with my son, I need to know where you come from."

"I can't say that my family is something that you would approve of. But I was raised proper, taught the ways of the royals because everyone has to learn, right? I am no longer with my family. I have no connection, no ties, no understanding of their lives now. That it is, again, by choice, one that I hope you and everyone here can respect. And if you cannot, I understand that as well."

The queen dropped her mask just slightly and asked the most direct question she could. "What are you running from?"

"Control. I'm running from those who seek to control my life." I straightened, lungs struggling beneath the corset. "Everyone deserves that basic right, but my family didn't agree. They wanted to control every aspect of my life, and I couldn't take it anymore."

"Do you not think they would be proud of you now?"

"Maybe, but I don't really care about making them proud right now."

"I understand." She sipped her tea, looking at me over the rim of the cup. But the way she looked at me told me she wouldn't be letting the matter go.

She smiled when I reached for the orange pastry in front of me. "I doubt it will be as good as yours. I'll have to try them someday, but I'll leave that for my son for now."

That line made my stomach hurt. If she ever asked to eat my food, I would have a serious problem; the mere thought made my stomach churn.

We finished our tea in silence, and despite my nausea, I forced myself to try the food. No wonder the other chefs were upset; their meticulously prepared dishes with their sweet and savory blend of flavors were being overshadowed by my exotic style. Their creations were airy and had a spark of flavor I knew I could never master on my own.

I remained with the queen until she was called away. That was the way it always was with the Royals. There was always something to be done, something to prepare for. I didn't hate it. In fact, I felt a weight lift from my shoulders the moment she left, and the silence of the room was a welcome change. I finished my tea and ate a few more of the treats, happy to eat something that I hadn't created myself before going back to my room.

Once there, I became very aware of how I existed in a space that wasn't really my own. Asante had told me he expected his mother to have already been looking into my past, and he was right. Though the queen was cordial, I had no hopes of her actually leaving it alone. Queen Toci wanted to know everything about me. I couldn't make it easier for her to find out who I was. There were echoes of me all around the room, which I quickly got to work erasing. The first step to protecting my secret was cleaning up anything that could lead her to finding out who I was.

My priority became cleaning up all shedding. Hair and scales. Though I hadn't shifted in a long time, I still shed like any other dragon. Especially in my sleep. I'd wake up and find scaly bits in my bed. Anything I found, I picked up and put in a small bag. I couldn't trust just tossing it into the trash bin for collection. I had to hide it all and dispose of it when I could.

While I cleaned, my mind drifted back to my family, and Asante's words came back to me. The way he talked of his brother. I couldn't help but wonder if my own sibling felt the same after I had gone. Did my younger sister inherit my responsibilities when I left home? Did she feel like Asante? Had she gone neglected in my presence? Did she hate me for my absence?

When I was done, I snuck out of my room. I needed fresh air and time to clear my mind. After some searching, I found myself back in the garden where Asante planned our picnic dinner. The space truly was beautiful, and I was happy to have the chance to take it all in, but with every step I took, I could feel someone's eyes on me.

The guards watched me carefully, and I made sure I did nothing worth reporting to the queen. Was that what it would be like to be with him? If I stayed with Asante, would I never have privacy? The questions fluttered through my mind, but I couldn't understand why they were there.

"It doesn't matter!" I muttered to myself. It didn't matter how it would be, because I had no plans on staying with him.

"Kiala," Uradis called out to me from the flowered arches standing at the entrance to the garden.

"Yes?" I turned to her after picking up a fallen flower.

"I finally found you." She walked over to me. "Prince Asante has returned, and he's requesting your presence."

"Oh." I look down at the dress I wore. I'd removed the corset while cleaning and never put it back on.

"You look beautiful," she reassured me. "Don't worry about it."

"Is that obvious?" I smirked.

"Why wouldn't you want to look good for him?" She winked at me. "Every woman wants to look good for their love."

I looked away from her when she said the word love. Asante wasn't my love. I didn't even like him that much. "I guess you're right."

She led me to the prince, who stood by a small pond at the opposite end of the grounds, close to where they kept the serabringers. In the distance, I could hear their excited neighing and wished we could visit them again.

"Another beautiful dress." Asante complimented me.

"Thank you." I placed my hand where the missing corset should have been. "I had tea with your mother this morning."

He pursed his lips. "How did that go?"

"Better than I expected." I smiled, hoping to reassure him. "She was sweet, inquisitive, but respectful."

"I'm glad to hear that." He sighed and dropped his head back as he looked out over the water. "I thought she might give you more trouble."

"It was okay, I promise." I placed my hand on his arm. "Are you alright? You look upset."

"There's a lot I need to get done in a short period." He walked over to a small clawfoot bench behind us. "Sit with me, please."

"I don't have any treats for you today." I smiled as I joined him. "There wasn't much time to make them after everything else."

"A slight disappointment, but I understand." He pouted. "My mother was a priority. You can make more for me tomorrow, right?"

"Of course I will."

"How's your ankle?" he looked down at my foot.

"It's perfect." I lifted my foot and rolled my ankle for him to see. "No pain at all."

"Good." He abruptly turned to me and pulled my hand into his. "Will you fly with me?"

The question came out of nowhere and left me choked with panic. "What?"

"I haven't gone on a flight in a while, you know. Let my dragon out." He pointed at the sky. "I think it would be good to relieve tension, but. I don't want to go on my own. Would you go with me?"

Even if flying wouldn't reveal who and what I really was, I wasn't ready for this step.

"Asante- I," I took a deep breath. "I don't know if that's a good idea." For a man and a woman to take flight together, it signified taking another step in their relationship. A paired flight strengthened the bond between a couple. Asante knew what he was asking. He was testing the waters, but I was not prepared to take that step with him.

"Why not?" He looked genuinely disappointed.

"You know what that means if we do that." Our eyes met. "Do you really want to go there knowing this isn't real?"

"Oh." He dropped my hand. "I'm sorry. Momentary lapse in judgment. I forgot what this is. Seeing you in the dress looking like you do right now. It was improper for me to ask that of you."

"It's alright." His apology felt hollow, a thin coverup for something more, but I didn't dare ask him to reveal it.

"If you won't fly with me, can I ask another favor of you?"

I chewed my lip before responding. "What is it?"

"We have some important guests coming, people we've been hoping to meet with for a long while. This is why my father has been away. Mending the relationship and they've finally agreed." He spoke with honor, clearly proud of what his father had accomplished. "Your food would be the perfect way to wrap up their visit."

"You want me to make treats for someone?" I gawked. I wasn't sure what I expected the favor to be, but it wasn't that.

"Yes. I know I said you were only here to make them for me, but this is a special occasion. It would be a little more work on your end, but I would truly appreciate it if you could do this."

"Of course. Who is it?" I perked up at the opportunity to talk about menus instead of flying.

"It's the King and Queen of Frostspire. It's been years since our people...."

He continued speaking, but I couldn't hear him over the sound of my heart dropping into my stomach.

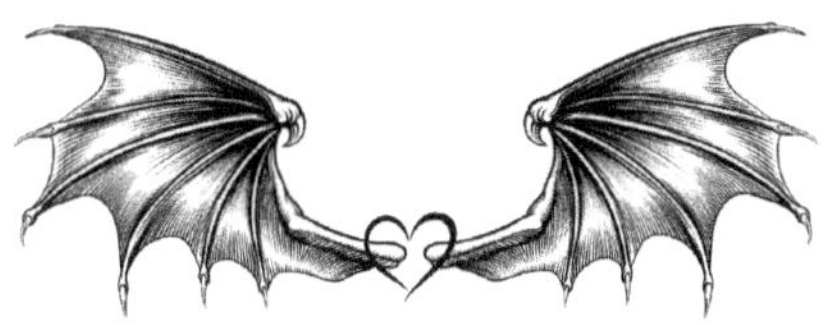

CHAPTER 10

"**I**'m sorry." I interrupted him once my racing heart slowed again. "Did you say the Frostspire royals are coming here?"

"Yes. The threat of the trolls is increasing, and we must work together if we are to remain strong."

"I see."

Asante noticed my trepidation. "Is there a reason you wouldn't want to make the treats for them?"

"Oh, I mean, I just..." I stammered, searching desperately for an excuse. "I've never made something for an event this important.

Wouldn't you want your chefs to do this? They're all so much more skilled than I am."

"I want them to have something unique, something that says we are changing for the better. Giving them our normal delights won't do that."

"This is really important to you, isn't it?"

"It is, but it's okay for you to say no. This isn't a part of our original bargain. You can just keep up appearances as we have been doing. It's working. Everyone believes we're in love."

"I'll do it." The confirmation fell out of my mouth before I could stop myself. Why was I being so agreeable?

"You will?" Asante sounded as shocked as I felt.

"Yes." Already I was thinking of ways to change my food so they wouldn't recognize it. "Wait, do I have to meet them?"

"No, you're not officially a part of the family. No one would expect you to attend such an important meeting."

"Great, I mean, it's enough pressure as it is just to be making the desserts."

"I understand. And I appreciate you doing this for me."

"It's for the betterment of our people, right? How could I say no to doing even a minor part to make that happen?"

He grabbed my hand again. "Thank you, Kiala."

"You're welcome." I nodded. "When are they coming?"

"Three nights from now. We just got word. Apparently, our side of the island isn't the only one the trolls visited."

A sudden, sharp pain shot through my stomach at the horrifying thought of trolls invading my home; the image of their grotesque faces flashed before my eyes followed by a deep feeling of guilt. I should have been there.

"That should be enough time." I tried to act as if timing was my only concern. But deep down, I had so much more to be worried about.

I spent the next two days preparing for the event. I locked myself away in my kitchen, making variations of my recipes, hoping to make them different enough so they wouldn't be recognizable, but not so much that Asante would question me about it. There were other questions that fluttered through my mind. Like how many people would I have to cook for? Would the king of Starwell also be there? Would other members of the royal family from Frostspire be there?

It didn't matter. Whoever attended the meeting wasn't my concern. I wouldn't have to be a part of it. All I had to do was bake sweets, hand them off to be served, and hide until the party ended.

If I could do that, I could avoid any drama.

Asante visited me the night before the event. I stood in the kitchen covered in flour and served him the best versions of my desserts. It was the first time I'd seen him since he asked me his favor. The smile stretched across my face as I watched his reaction to the food. He could be mad at me later if he didn't like how the variations tasted during the meeting.

"They are going to love these." He smiled and licked the fragranced cream from his lips.

"I hope so." I smiled nervously.

"You're being modest. You know they will." He looked around the kitchen. "You've really made this space your own. Are you sure this is okay for you?"

"It's perfect, cozy and quiet." I smiled. "Thank you again for giving me this space to work in."

"Of course. I want you to be comfortable here."

I thought about what his uncle had said to me. Asante was a softy beneath the tough exterior.

"I hope everything goes well tomorrow." I wiped down the table between us as if I hadn't already cleaned it twice before he came.

"You need to relax." He grabbed my hand, stopping the frantic motion. "Come on."

"What?" I frowned as he stood and led me to the door.

"Let's go for a walk." He looked back at me. "It will be good for both of us."

This time, we strolled through an unfamiliar part of their property. The sounds of birdsong filled the air. Moonlight from Rhyxis, the moon rumored to guide the subconscious, bathed the grounds, casting long shadows and creating an ethereal glow. Lunaterra had thirteen moons, all representing different faiths and practices. My favorite was Sylvos. It was the moon of the forests where I had often daydreamed about running off to live.

But I had to stay in the present, which made me think of Asante's requests.

It felt even heavier thinking of the timing. It was a special time of year when new mates showcased their love. And because of that, dragons flew together in pairs, creating dancing spirals above our heads.

"Don't worry." Asante nudged me with his shoulder. "I won't ask you to fly with me again."

A nervous chuckle slipped from my lips. "I appreciate that."

"I bet your dragon is beautiful." He said, and my stomach fluttered.

"Asante-,"

"Sorry." He held his hand up. "Dropping it now."

"You're acting like you like me." I teased him.

"Am I?" He glanced at me.

"This is supposed to be a mutual arrangement, like a business deal. You're not supposed to like me."

"Well, maybe you should make it harder to like you." He stepped away from me and I followed him.

"How can I do that?" I asked. "Tell me and I'll do it."

"I'm not sure." Asante looked at me and his eyes darkened for a moment. "What if it's not possible?"

"Maybe I can start making the desserts bad again." I shifted the tone. "I could go back to making them how I did when I first got here."

"Don't you dare." Asante reached out, pulling me closer to him.

I gasped as my chest pressed against his. "What are you doing?"

"Breaking the rules." He took a deep breath, then lowered his face to mine.

"Asante." I pulled back just a little, but not enough to break his hold.

"Will you hit me?" His brow raised.

"I-,"

A smirk lifted at the corner of his lips. "It'll be worth it."

He kissed me again. That time was different. As his lips lingered against mine, there was no pain to counteract the feelings. There was nothing to distract me from the taste of him, the way my body responded to him. And there was nothing to drown out the screaming voice in my head.

Oh god, I like him!

~*~

The next night, I sat nervously in my room after making hundreds of pastries and handing them off to the staff, who would serve them to the royals. The urge to run away, to disappear where no one could ever find me, gnawed at me constantly. That was the perfect solution. If they couldn't find me, there would be no way to mistakenly encounter their guests. Asante gave me his word. I wouldn't have to go to the party, but my intuition gnawed at me to take further precautions. I ignored that feeling, choosing to trust what he said and headed for bed.

I had just pulled the covers back on the bed when I heard the excited chatter of women approaching my door. Panic had me looking at the window. Could I jump out without breaking my neck? The answer was no.

Knock, knock, knock.

Time was up.

"Yes?" I opened the door as if unaware of why they were there.

"Your sweets were a hit! They can't stop talking about them." The woman entered my room and pulled the cloak from my shoulders. "I hope you aren't leaving. They want to meet you!"

"Meet me?" I panicked. "No, I can't."

"What do you mean, you can't?" She reached for me, ready to start her work. "Now, let's just fix your hair and change your dress!"

The walls felt like they were closing in on me and I backed away from the woman, swatting her hands away from me. "Stop, don't touch me."

My lungs felt ready to explode in my chest. I sat on my bed and gasped for air. "I can't do this!"

"Are you okay?" she asked, her voice heavy with worry. "I'll get help!"

The woman ran out of the room, leaving me alone. I stood only to close the door behind her and placed my back against it. Maybe this was the solution. Freak out and stay in my room until it was over.

"Kiala? Are you okay?"

My plan to stay hidden went out the window, as Asante's voice called out from the other side of the door. How could I ignore him? Would he go away even if I asked him to?

"I'm fine." I called out.

"Please open the door." His voice sounded strange. "I can tell something is wrong. Please let me in."

I should have ignored him. I should have told him to go away, but I didn't. Instead, I stood, wiped the tears from my face, and opened the door. Before I saw his face, I turned and walked away, allowing him to enter behind me.

"What happened?"

"Nothing. I didn't expect-," the pain in my chest returned as I struggled to catch my breath. "I'm sorry Asante, I just can't go out there. They want me to, but I can't."

"Are you afraid?" He looked at me like he wanted to shield me from the world. "Do you think someone will hurt you?"

His question had the walls moving in again. "It's not that, I just can't. I don't want to see them."

"Then you don't have to." He didn't question me any further. "Don't worry about it. Don't get yourself upset like this."

"But the queen." Finally, I took a deep breath. "Your mother will be upset if I don't go."

"She'll understand and if she doesn't, she can be mad at me. I'm the one who said you wouldn't have to do this." He grabbed my cloak the woman had draped on the chair and wrapped it around me. "Let's go."

"Where are you taking me?" I looked up at him as he tied the hood around my neck.

"Away from here." He smiled. "What I should have done before this started."

"You can't leave. The meeting isn't over." I wiped the tears from my eyes, suddenly sobering up. "It won't look good if you do."

"Kiala, please." He touched my cheek. "Just let me do this."

He led me outside to the stables where the serabringers were. I thought we would take them for a ride again, but Asante detoured away from the doors and instead led me to the field at the side of it.

"I know you won't shift into your dragon and fly with me. I respect your choice, but at least let me carry you."

He didn't wait for my protest. Asante turned his back to me. He stripped away his clothing, placing them neatly into the bag he carried for that purpose. He secured the strap around his leg. Designed to stretch with his growing form, the strap sat loose against his skin. After one last glance at me, he transformed, the air crackling with energy as his human form shifted into a magnificent dragon. The dragon's beauty was breathtaking; his scales gleamed, and his powerful wings caught the fading light. The varying shades of emerald on his scales were like a thousand tiny gems reflecting the light, some dark and others so bright they seemed to glow. My favorite color.

He lowered his neck, allowing me to climb onto his back. He nudged me with his wide nose to tell me to hold on. I gripped my hands in the hair that ran down the back of his long neck and allowed Asante to carry me away.

I buried my face in Asante's neck as he carried me. The deafening whoosh of his wings was almost overwhelming, but beneath it, I could feel the steady, powerful rhythm of his heart. It was a powerful, steady beat, and as I pressed my ear against him, his pulse resonated like a drum against my skin, a rhythmic soundtrack to our flight. Instead of looking at the lands that passed beneath us, I closed my eyes and listened to his heart.

I tried to hide my disappointment when he finally landed. He perched carefully on a cliff overlooking the fire dragon territory, lowering his head to let me get down from his back safely. I placed the knotted ball of his clothes at his feet, then turned my back to give him privacy to redress. While he dressed, I took in the view. I could see out all the way to the ocean. I didn't realize what I was searching for until I didn't see it. The sails of troll ships. Where were they?

"I figured you would like it." Asante joined me, unaware of what thoughts raced through my mind. "This is one of my favorite spots."

"It's breathtaking." I swallowed my concerns. "You come here a lot?"

"Yes, not as much as I used to, though."

I turned to further inspect the cliff and noticed the opening to a small cave. "What's this?"

Asante stepped in front of me. "Before you go in, promise not to judge me."

"Why would I judge you?" I pushed him aside and walked into the cave and gasped when I saw what he tried to hide. "Asante!"

I had never seen an actual dragon hoard before. Most people would never have one, and if they did, they kept it a secret. Inside the cave was Asante's hoard. A massive collection of items, some worth more than I could calculate and others holding only sentimental value.

"You said you wouldn't judge me." He held his finger up.

"I said no such thing." I corrected him. "This is a lot to take in."

"Well, don't please." He dropped his head and pretended to pout. "It is my shame. You can't make fun of me for it."

"You really take this dragon thing seriously, don't you?" I laughed. "Just like the old dragons, flying around and gathering things to hoard."

"I know we're supposed to have evolved past this, but I can't help it." He threw his hands up. "I love my things. My mother hated it. She tried everything she could to get me to stop. And as far as she knows, I did. I found this place a long time ago. The only one who knew about it was my brother, and he swore to keep my secret safe."

"It's kind of cute." I laughed as I moved around the space cataloging the different jewels, tapestries and other trinkets. "Thinking of you as a child doing this. And besides, now I know your dirty little secret."

"Will you use it to blackmail me?" he asked. "What would people think if they found out their future king did this?"

"Maybe?" I tapped my chin with my finger. "I mean, I could definitely use this for leverage. I'm not sure for what yet."

"That's not fair," he groaned. "At least let me know the bargain now."

"I think it is." I started going through the piles of odds and ends. "There really is no reason behind any of this, is there?"

"I go through phases." He chuckled and pointed to a stack of gray rocks. "Like that, for two years, I was obsessed with the stones at the edge of the ocean. I would sneak down there by myself to gather as many as I could."

"And no one ever caught you?" I pointed to the stack of plants at the back wall of the cave. "That couldn't have been easy to sneak up here."

"If they did, they didn't speak about it." He shrugged. "Maybe they knew and ignored it. I wasn't supposed to be their king. They may have just assigned me the eccentric brother tag like they did my uncle."

"Thank you for sharing this." I turned to him. "It's funny, yes, but I get how difficult this must have been for you to trust me with."

"It was worth the risk if it made you feel better. Did it?"

I nodded. "Actually, it does."

"Good. Then I guess you can make fun of me about it."

Asante found two cushions in his stash that were from a royal party. He said he hoped to gather more but couldn't. After giving me the backstory of his ploy to take the cushions, he sat them at the opening of the cave and helped me sit on one before taking the other for himself. We sat, looking out at the night sky and inhaling the salty scent of ocean air as the cool breeze brushed across our skin.

"I'm not supposed to feel this way about you." Asante finally broke the silence.

I looked at him. "What?"

"I can't help it Kiala, I keep trying to correct my thinking. I know this arrangement between us isn't real. But there is something about you I can't get away from."

"It's the food." I nudged him. "Once I'm gone, you won't have it anymore. It will fade."

"It really isn't." He shook his head. "I considered that, but it's not true."

A sudden rush of heat surged through me, and my heart pounded in my chest. "It isn't?"

"It's you, Kiala." Asante shifted in his seat to look me in the eye. He grabbed my hand to pull me closer. "It was you before I knew you could cook. Before the first time you slapped me or put me in my place. It was you when I first saw you."

"When I fell?" I laughed. "How could that possibly be the moment?"

He chuckled. "I saw you long before that. Hidden behind those old ladies, wrapped in a scarf. It was your eyes that caught me. The way you were clearly judging me and everyone else around me. I was making my way to you before you fell. That's how I got to you so quickly."

"Asante." I tried to stop him, but he continued.

"It's you. And I think that's what makes your food so intoxicating to me." He lifted my fingers to his lips. "These are the hands that make the love you put into your food. I feel it in every bite."

"Love?"

"It isn't love for me, it's the essence of who you are. You are love, Kiala. I can tell." He kissed my fingertips. "I want to earn your love. I want to deserve your heart."

"You're going to kiss me again, aren't you?" I asked when he looked at me with those dark eyes.

"You're going to let me," he inched closer, and slipped his arm around my waist. "Aren't you?"

I nodded slowly, the anticipation building with every inch, only stopping when his lips pressed against mine.

Under the moonlight, surrounded by his hoard, our kiss deepened. It may have been improper, but at that moment, none of that mattered. Asante's hand caressed my back, and my hands found his neck and head. I massaged the back of his neck as he pulled me to his lap. After a moment of hesitation, as our eyes met and our breath caught, we returned to our kiss.

"I want more of you." Asante spoke, his kiss moving from my lips to my chin.

I dropped my head back and pushed my hips against him, a gentle encouragement. I wanted more, but I couldn't say the words. He did no more. His kiss lingering, needing more from me. So, I pulled back from him, just enough to allow the moonlight to wash against the skin between us, as I slipped my hand between our bodies and confidently stroked him through his pants. I held his gaze as I moved my hand, encouraging the growth beneath my palm. That was all he needed. Asante shifted his weight, pulling a blanket from a dark corner stacked with fabric. He laid it out on the cave floor, then lowered me onto it.

"Are you sure?" he asked.

"Yes." I said, breath heavy with anticipation.

"Your first time should be special, Kiala."

"How innocent of you," I smiled, returning my hand to the place between his legs.

He groaned and slammed his lips against mine. Lowering his weight on top of me as he did.

He paused as if he would ask me again. Was I ready? Was this what I wanted? My mind felt cloudy, but my body was ready to accept him.

I lifted my back from the ground, wrapping my arms around his neck to pull him closer. How could I convey to him that I wanted him? This could be the only chance we had. Soon I would fly away from my home for good, and I would take the memory of him with me.

As we kissed, his body warmed. That inner fire revealing how much he reciprocated my sentiments. As our kiss intensified, we undressed. Slowly pulling back layers of fabric to reveal our flesh. I blushed when the quick exhale crossed his lips when my breast were exposed to the moonlight. Chills spread across my skin when he pulled the dress over my hips and down my legs. The back of his fingers left a heated trail across my body.

Asante admired me. With each moment that passed, I felt more like a work of art than a woman longing for his touch. I lay bare to the world as he kneeled beside me. Then he grabbed my foot, bringing my toes to his lips, and gently kissed them before moving up to my ankle.

"Praise the gods," he moaned the first religious sentiment I'd heard from him.

My back arched when his lips met my knee. My thighs spread, urging him to go further. And moments later, I gripped the blanket beneath us as Asante tasted me. I imagined my pastries in his hands, the sweet jelly on his lips as he coaxed me to the edge. How many ways could I feed him?

His lips left me, and my body seized with frustration. I wanted more from him. But I had to be patient, just like with my dough. I needed to give it time to rise.

Asante was an artist, painting my body with his kisses and brushes from his fingers. Again, he lowered his chest to mine, putting just enough of his weight on me to spread my legs. His hand slipped beneath my back and he positioned his dick against me. Just as he entered, he capture me with a kiss so passionate it took my breath away. I gasped as I accepted him.

He was warm, unlike the ice dragons I'd had before. It didn't take time for him to heat up. He started hot and only got hotter. And the more his temperature rose, the more I felt the ice inside me thaw. Was this the fear our ancestors had? Would his fire kill my ice? Just as I decided it didn't matter, I felt his lips shiver against mine.

"Are you okay?" I spoke with a soft gasp as he continued his slow strokes.

"Never better." He grinned.

"You're shivering." I smiled, lifting my hips to accept more of him. "Maybe we should stop. It's cold in here. I don't want you to get sick."

"That won't happen." He growled. "I'm fine."

I wrapped my arms around his neck and felt the sizzle of my newfound heat against the cool of his body. Our energy had entwined and, as we continued, the cave filled with our steam.

Does he know? Why didn't he want to stop? Is this okay?

Those thoughts flittered through my mind, but as quickly as they came, they faded away. Asante's heat returned to him. The shivering stopped, and he continued to take me.

That night, underneath the moonlight, ignoring the world and all the problems that awaited, I gave myself to Asante.

Time and time again.

CHAPTER 11

My head rested on Asante's chest as I listened to his heart again. It sounded different from when he was in his dragon form. Less of a thunder pulse and more of a soft drumming. Still, the warmth of his flesh melted the ice I'd built around myself. I realized, as I inhaled the mixed scent of salty air and the musk from his body, that I no longer wanted to leave Asante. But how could I not?

"We should head back now." Asante's voice startled me.

"I wish we didn't have to." The words slipped out of my mouth before I could process the thoughts behind them. I smacked my hand over my mouth.

"Don't worry. I won't tell anyone." He kissed the top of my head before sitting up.

I dressed as Asante headed outside to shift into his dragon. Again, with his clothing tied to my side, I climbed onto his back and let him carry me. Even after our intimate moment, I couldn't show him my dragon and he didn't ask. Maybe he thought in time I would soften to the idea. We had just taken a big step. How much longer could I keep that side of myself from him?

As he carried me back to his home, it became harder to deny how much I liked him. Especially after what we had done. It wasn't often I let anyone touch me, let alone taste me the way he had. The longing to be with him was only growing, but that feeling was echoed by a thought that made my heart ache. How could I be with him if he didn't know everything about me?

I made it into my room without being seen, or at least without being confronted. How long would it be before the walls were whispering about the couple running away from the palace? Were they already talking about how I freaked out about meeting the king and queen of Frostspire? Did it even matter?

After cleaning myself up, I lay in the bed and stare out the window at the sky.

How did it come to this?

A few hours later, when the birds were singing their morning song, Asante returned to me. I stood fully dressed, my apron already on, ready to head to my kitchen, when a sharp knock echoed at the door.

"What are you doing?" the prince asked me when I opened my door.

"I have to work. Remember, I must bake treats for the prince." I winked at him. "It's the only thing I do around here."

"Not today." He grabbed my hand. "You're coming with me."

"Don't you have things to take care of?" I laughed. "You're a prince with important duties to tend to."

"What could be more important than this?" Asante lifted my hand to his lips. "I can't think of one thing."

As I followed Asante back to the serabringer stables, I decided to confide in him completely. It felt more important to tell him everything than to keep my secret. And maybe, if I explained it all, he would understand why I couldn't stay with him, why the weight of unspoken words had become too much to bear. I only hoped that he wouldn't hold it against me for not telling him earlier.

Either way, I would keep it together until our deal was done. Then I would leave him, just as I promised I would.

Asante pulled the same creatures from their stables and Synth greeted me as if we were old friends. She tapped her hooves on the ground and neighed softly as she nuzzled my neck.

"She really likes you!" Asante spoke.

"You think so?" I brushed her head with my hand.

"Yes, but I get it." Asante stepped over to me and kissed me quickly on the cheek. "I do too."

"You're going to love our herd. They're of the purest breed!"

I froze at the sound of the boisterous voice. He sounded just like Asante, his voice only more tinged by the weight of time.

Please, no. Don't let it be! Panic seized me instantly; my breath hitched, and my mind raced. Footsteps approached as I searched for a place to hide. Asante, seemingly unfazed by my rising panic, continued on grooming the serabringer.

"Oh, he looks for any reason to show these things off!" Queen Toci's unmistakable voice rang out.

"I'm proud of them. They deserve the praise. Besides, I know the serabringers in Frostspire differ from the ones we have here. How long has it been since you've seen our breed? We should exchange notes!"

Before I could run and hide, those voices were right on top of us. And a moment after my heart fell to my stomach, Queen Toci shattered my hopes for escape.

"Asante, there you are, my son."

"Where did you get off to last night?" the deep voice of the king asked.

Startled, I slipped away from Asante and hid behind Synth. "Give me cover, girl." I whispered to her.

Synth, who seemed to love me moments before, stepped away from me and I scurried closer to her. "Please. Remember, you like me!"

The serabringer huffed as if put off by my sudden display of desperation.

"I'll bring you treats!" I offered the bribe I wasn't sure would work and then, as if I'd uncovered the secret to her heart, she spread her wings as if she understood exactly what I needed.

"I had something to take care of." Asante offered. "I apologize for not returning to the festivities."

"It's alright, things were pretty much done as it were." His father sounded warm, less abrasive than his mother. "Is that your love?"

"Um,"

"Love is a big statement to make when they haven't even declared it." His mother corrected his father's assumption. Of course she would. She didn't think I was deserving of her son. "We must be interrupting. But since we're here, dear the Queen and King of Frostpire would love to meet you," she said. "This is the woman who crafted those delicious treats last night."

"Oh, I would love to meet her." Hiding behind Synth, I heard a voice I hadn't heard since running away from home. Soft, motherly, and it made my heart break. It was my plan to never see her again, to never face her disappointment.

There was nowhere to go, though. And before I knew it, Asante's mother had shuffled around Synth, grabbed my arm and pulled me out of hiding. Synth stretched her wings, trying to keep me hidden but it didn't work. And the moment I was in clear view, the queen of Frostspire clutched her chest.

"Oh, it can't be." Tears instantly flowed down her face, and I reached for her but pulled back. It was not my place to comfort her.

"Kiala?" The king of the ice dragons stepped closer to me. "Is that you?"

I said nothing.

"You know her?" The king of Starwell asked. His eyes darted between Asante and me. "Asante?"

It wasn't Asante who answered the question.

"This is our daughter." My mother reached for my father, pulling him back from me.

"We met your daughter last night. You said you sent her home ahead of you." Asante's mother looked furious. "What do you mean, this is your daughter? Are you playing some kind of joke on us?"

"This is our eldest," my father said softly, then his tone changed to anger when he spoke to me. "We thought you were dead! What are you doing here?"

Panic had me choking on my words, and foolishly I looked to Asante for help. He looked just as hurt as everyone else.

"Is this true?" He asked me.

"I can't do this." I tugged on Synth's wing pleading for her to cooperate with me. She did not.

"Kiala?" Asante stepped closer to me.

"Don't do this, Asante." I tried again to get Synth to take me on her back, but she moved away from me, further exposing me to the people who surrounded me.

"You're just going to run away?"

"I would if Synth would cooperate!" I nudge her. "Come on, girl."

"She's not going to because I haven't told her to." Asante asserted. And it was like Synth took that as a challenge. Hers was a spirit wanting to be free, just like my own.

Synth lowered her wing, an offer of help in protest of the man who claimed to tell her what to do. I placed one foot on the wing, and she lifted me onto her back. With a last glance back, I found Asante's face. He looked more confused than anyone else there. "Go." I whispered to Synth, and she took off running.

Synth's footfalls were echoed by another's. I didn't have to look back to see who it was. Every time Synth sped up, so did Kune. He was like her shadow, matching every stride she took. And when he caught up, pulling his rider to my side, I kept my eyes forward. I couldn't look at him.

Asante didn't call out to me. He rode alongside me in silence until Synth came to a stop just beneath the same tree she did the last time I rode her. I hopped from her back and ran for the path into the wooded area where I fell into Asante's arms.

"Kiala, stop!" Asante chased after me. But I ignored his call and ran until my lungs burned from the effort.

"Why are you doing this? Stop running!"

"I can't I have to keep running." I doubled over, gasping for air but keeping my back to him. "No, I can't stop."

"What is this?" He demanded. "Tell me they're wrong. They have to be mistaking you for someone else."

"If I told you that now, would you believe it?"

"You're really their daughter?" I heard him move closer to me, but he stopped. "Kiala, just tell me, please."

"Asante, please." I wanted him to leave me alone with my shame, but he refused.

"Talk to me, Kiala. Help me understand this." He tried to mask the pain he felt, but his voice trembled in an unfamiliar way. This was the first time I'd heard him be truly unsure of himself.

"I am the promise born." I turned to face him as I spoke. "That's what they call it in Frostspire. First born to the king and queen, next in line to rule."

"You are?" there was hope in the question. He wanted me to tell him I wasn't who they said I was. This was the last grasp at preserving what reluctantly grew between us.

"Yes." I crushed that hope.

"Why would you hide something like this?" Asante stepped back from me. "How could you lie about who you are?"

"You talked about how it sucked to be second born. How your brother overshadowed you. Did you never think about running away from that?" I swallowed my emotions. "I was first born, Asante. Thrust into a life predetermined for me. Nothing about my life was a choice I could make for myself. From how I spent my time as a child to who I would eventually marry. My parents had it all mapped out before I said my first words."

"You could have told me." He shook his head. "I would have understood."

"I was going to tell you, Asante." I paced. "If this hadn't happened, I would have told you myself."

"When, Kiala? When were you going to tell me?" He turned away from me for a moment, as if regaining his composure. When he looked at me, I could see the hurt he tried to bury behind a mask of anger. "You know it is impossible for us to be together. Fire dragons and ice dragons aren't supposed to do this! Why would you let me share so much of myself with you?"

"I didn't ask for this, remember? You forced me to be here."

"Right, so I'm to blame for your dishonesty?"

"That's not what I mean. The point isn't to place blame."

"You're to blame, Kiala. Do you not see how you're accountable for this? Your people thought you died! Your family, your sister!" He shouted. "Did you ever stop to think about her? Did you think about how she would feel without you? Have you imagined what her life must have been like without her brother there by her side?"

"Her brother?" I frowned at him and then it hit me. Asante's rage wasn't for my people or my sister, it was for him. For the loss he felt when his brother died. "Asante-," I stopped when he held his hand up to me.

"Prince Asante." He corrected me. "To you, I am Prince Asante."

"Wow. So, everything just stops now?" My eyes burned with unshed tears. "I understand that you're hurt right now. And I get how this makes you feel, especially after everything you've been through. I should have seen that before, but does that erase everything? How you felt about me? That ends?"

"You're not who I thought you were." His jaw tightened as he looked at me. "The person I thought you were would never lie about something like this."

"You knew nothing about me." I pointed at him. "You saw me and decided I was the one for you before you even knew my name. You held me to a standard in your mind long before I would have ever been able to show you who I am. And now, because I made a choice to take ownership of my own path, you're judging me again? You don't know what my life was like. You have no idea how hard it was for me to walk away from everything! How can you stand here and talk to me like this?"

"I should have let my mom continue with her search." It looked like Asante was ready to cry but he held it back.

"What do you mean?"

"I stopped her. Caught her aides leaving your room with things and I told her to back off." He paced for a moment. "She was going to have my uncle look into you. That's what he used to do, find the things no one else could. If I hadn't talked her out of it-,"

"You did that?"

"Yes, because I felt you deserved your privacy. Had I known this is what you were hiding from me, I wouldn't have stood in the way. You should have told me!" He swallowed back his emotions. "This wouldn't have been this way."

"Don't say that." I corrected him. "If I had told you before, you would have judged me just like you are now. You would have sent me back to Frostpire to build a bridge with my parents. Right? Isn't that why they're here now? Do you think you would have hesitated to use me as a pawn in this?"

"Don't do that. Don't tell me what I would have done. I told you I knew you were for me before you first spoke to me. I wouldn't have sent you away like that!"

"If it was me, if what you felt was real, wouldn't you offer me some understanding now instead of treating me like this?"

"Release me from the promise." He didn't bother answering my question.

"What?"

"Release me, Kiala." He repeated. "I made a promise to you. I can no longer keep that promise. It is not fair to lay my life down on your lie."

"Okay. You're right." I looked down at my hand and for the first time in years, I spoke to my dragon. She responded eagerly and the familiar sensation of tingles spread across my hand. Within moments, my fingers stretched and the dragon claws appeared. With teary eyes, I bared my chest and looked Asante in the eye. "Prince Asante, I release you from your dragon's promise."

I dragged the tip of the claw across my chest, spilling my own blood.

With a tightened jaw, Asante turned his back to me. "There is no need for you to stay here anymore. Everyone knows you're a liar. Just go."

And then he walked away.

I stood there, watching him until he was out of sight. And then I heard the hooves of one serabringer leave. After my tears stopped, I returned to find Synth waiting for me. She lowered her head to nuzzle my chest, where the wound healed slowly.

"You like me again?" I patted her head, and she snorted. "Alright, let's go back. I have to face this."

Synth lifted me to her back. That could have been my chance to run away, to leave the stench of betrayal and the weight of guilt behind. But how many times would I have to do that? And my family knew I was alive now. I knew my mother would search for me. I had to face this, if only for a chance to end it the right way.

Before we made it there, I looked up to see Asante flying above me.

"Follow him." I whispered to Synth.

It was good I did, because it wasn't long after we started trailing him that the large boulder ripped through the air and hit Asante, knocking him from the sky.

CHAPTER 12

Synth couldn't run fast enough for me. Even with the boost from her wings, my mind couldn't fathom taking any longer to get to him. I wanted to call my dragon to the surface, but I was afraid. What if whatever attacked him took aim at me? I had to be smarter.

Why was there no one there with him? I knew the answer to the question that repeated in my mind. This was my fault. He wouldn't have been alone if he wasn't trying to escape me.

When we reached him, Asante lay in the middle of a field. The tall grass crushed by his dragon left him exposed in the center after his body shifted back. I jumped from Synth's back before she came to a complete stop, no longer concerned with being attacked.

"Asante!" I called out to him as I ran to his side.

His body was slick with blood, his eyes were swollen shut, and his skin burned with fever when I touched him. I looked away from him just long enough to survey the area. There was no obvious threat, no one there to continue harming him. When I lifted his head to my chest, he coughed, but the sound was weak, hollow.

"No, I have to get you back." I looked at Synth and realized there was no way she would move fast enough. So, I gave her an order. "Go home, girl."

She neighed softly, tilting her head in uncertainty.

"We'll be okay. Go." I encouraged her.

Synth backed away from me slowly, but when I called to my dragon, I could tell she felt the response the moment I did. And as Synth ran from home, my dragon emerged. For the first time in too long, she was free, but I had no time to survey myself. Asante was in trouble. His life on the line. I gently picked his body up into my hold and took flight.

As I flew to his home, staring down at the ground, I saw them. Trolls, running from the scene.

It was unbelievable how tiring it was to fly. My tired wings carried us right into the courtyard, where the guards met us with prejudice. I was an ice dragon flying into their territory. It was a wonder I wasn't shot down. Maybe they recognized the prince. It didn't matter. We landed safely, and I quickly laid him down.

Any threat I posed became secondary as they rushed to help him.

"Move aside!" I looked up, still in my dragon form, to see his uncle running toward us. He dropped to Asante's side and checked his vitals. Then he looked up at me. "Thank you."

I nodded.

"Take him to the infirmary. Carefully!" He directed the others, then turned to me, took off the long jacket he wore and laid it on the ground in front of me before turning and walking away to give me privacy to return to my form.

I hadn't even considered my clothing when I shifted. If I turned back, I would be exposed to the world. I picked up the coat, moved behind the trees nearby, and completed the painful shift back. It always hurt to shift after avoiding it for so long.

"Ah!" I cried out as I tried to pull the jacket over my arm. My muscles were on fire.

"Let me help."

I looked over my shoulder to find Uradis standing there.

"Thank you."

Regardless of my trepidation, I allowed Uradis to help me. Once the jacket was around me, she handed me a pair of soft slippers. "Figured you might want these."

"Why are you being so nice to me?" I asked.

"Bringing our people together. Remember? She pushed the slippers toward me and I took them as she lowered her voice to continue. "The prince threw his weight around. That's not your fault."

"Thank you, Uradis."

"Now, come with me. I'll bring you to Asante. His uncle wants to talk to you."

"Oh, okay. Whatever he needs."

Uradis led me to the healer's building. Instead of the small room where they kept me, Asante was in a large space. Three guards stood outside the door and to the left of them were four empty chairs.

"Sit here." Uradis told me before leaving. A few moments later, she returned, gave a small nod to the guards, and sat next to me. "They'll let us know when you can go inside."

I said nothing, though her words sparked new concern. Should I even be there at all? Would he want me with him?

That was when time slowed down. Sitting there wondering about what would happen. Each moment stretched on infinitely as my mind created countless variations of what would come. I pictured Asante coming out of the room on his own and telling me to leave. I imagined his uncle telling me he didn't make it. There were even thoughts of the queen, who I couldn't believe wasn't already there waiting to see her son. Just as I was about to ask

Uradis about the queen, the door opened and a woman I didn't recognize walked out into the hall.

"You can come in now," she said.

Uradis touched my hand. "Go ahead, I'll wait here."

I entered the room, painted red with gold drapes over the windows. In the middle of the room was a bed and on the bed was Asante. The swelling that covered his face and body had gone down, but in its place were fresh bruises. I tiptoed closer to him, but he wasn't conscious. I could have screamed his name, but he wouldn't have responded.

Next to his bed was a plush chair. I crossed the room, carefully scanning his body as I did and sat by his side. What else was I supposed to do? After a while, I couldn't take the silence anymore. So, instead of watching him breathe, I talked to him. I told him all the things I wanted to say before my secret was revealed.

"Asante, I know you likely can't hear me right now." I reached for his hand then hesitated, folding my hands together in my lap. "And I know that you never wanted to see me again. I just had to make sure you were okay. So, as soon as I know that you're okay, I will leave. You have my word, though I doubt that means much to you now. I wish you could hear me. Because I plan to tell you everything."

I glanced around the room. Though we were alone, I knew the walls had ears. There were guards outside the door and aides that were never too far away. Could any of them be listening?. It didn't matter if they knew the truth or not. The rumors would be louder than any truth I told.

"After the night we spent together," I continued talking to Asante. "I had made my mind up that you deserve to know the truth. And yes, you should have known everything about me before that happened. But you were never supposed to find your way into my heart. But you did. And as much as it hurts, I knew I had to tell you.

You asked me how I could leave and let everyone think the worst had happened to me. Leaving home was the hardest decision I ever had to make. But I made that decision because the future that was given to me was not the one I wanted. I made that choice not just because I didn't want to be there, but because our people deserved someone who did." I paused.

"I worried about my sister, but deep down, I think she would make a better ruler than me. She never outright said it, but I know Leah dreamed of being queen. She would talk so proudly about how she wanted to care for our people and elevate our status in the world. It was her passion and though they tried to teach me to love it, she came to it naturally. When I realized what our futures looked like. Two sisters denied what they wanted for themselves. I stepped out of the way." The smile lifted the corner of my lips when I thought of my sister. I had spent so much time worrying about my parents that I often forgot to consider her. "There's no doubt in my mind that she will do a wonderful job as queen. Though I still wonder if I should have asked her what she wanted. I guess, in a way, I'm just like my parents. I assumed she wanted the path I did not. Asante, I will leave your home. But I will not return to my own. That isn't fair to my sister or my people.

If I go back home, my parents will push me back into that role without a second thought, and that is not fair to Leah. My people deserve a queen who wants to be their queen, and that is not me. It never was. Yes, I care for them, but that's not the person I am. I watched my mother closely. For years, I saw how she gave up what she really wanted for herself in order to rule. And I realize how selfless of an act that is. The truth is, I am not that selfless." I dropped my head as if he could witness my shame.

"I wanted to live my life like my father. Full of passion and happiness and laughs that made his entire body shake. So yes, I left. Maybe I could have done it in a better way, but you know how this is. There's no way to walk away from the life we were born into. I had to make them think there was no way I could ever come back. So, I came up with a plan to fake an accident. As far as they knew, I fell off a cliff and into the ocean.

Once I knew they believed it, I came here. My mother would search for me, but Starwell would be the last place my mother, the King and Queen of the Ice Dragons, would ever think of finding their daughter." A soft chuckle escaped my lips. "The funny thing is that I didn't plan on staying here much longer. I was counting down until I had enough money saved to flee the island for good. Then you came into my shop, and everything changed."

I paused my confession and wondered how much more to tell him. Did it even make sense to keep going? Asante made it clear he didn't want me in his life anymore. As I looked at him, I realized I didn't want to change his mind. I only wanted him to understand me. And that was a selfish thing.

"None of this really matters, does it?" I felt the tears building in my eyes but kept them from falling. Finally, I lifted his hand into mine. "Just get better. Please. Your time with me may not be one of your favorites to look back on. But heal and get better to live long enough to regret it. And please know that I never will."

"How touching."

My attention snapped to the doorway where Domin stood with a disinterested expression, rolling his eyes.

"What are you doing here?" I dropped Asante's hand and stood as Domin approached me.

"I should ask you that. Do you really think we're gonna believe that story?" He laughed. "I heard it all. You ran away from home because you didn't want to be queen? That makes no sense. Many would kill to be in your position. And now? Is it just a coincidence that you're here when our prince is injured?"

"You can't think I did this." I pointed at Asante. "I brought him here. Why would I hurt him only to bring him back to be healed?"

"Maybe this is all a ploy to throw us off." He stepped around to the side of Asante's bed. "Here you are, the ice princess, baking your poisonous sweets for our prince. Weakening him and making him fall for you until he lets his guard down. And now, just look what you've done."

"I did not do this." I insisted. "Why would I hurt him? I had no reason to!"

"Then who else did it?" Domin spit the question at me.

"Kiala." My name crossed Asante's lip in a dry whisper.

"I knew it." Domin reached across the bed and pointed his ashy finger in my face.

"You knew what?" I slapped his hand away. "All he did was say my name. That's not a proclamation of my guilt."

"Or did he tell us the person who hurt him?" Domin narrowed his eyes. "I asked a question, and he answered."

"For the last time, I am not the one who did this." I shook my head. "You care so much about him, but instead of investigating this, you're accusing me."

"You're so smart, you claim you aren't the one," he lifted his chin. "Prove your innocence. Tell me who did it."

I felt a surge of panic, then recalled the sight of the fleeing trolls, their grotesque forms retreating as I carried Asante to safety. "Trolls!" I blurted out.

"Trolls?" He scoffed.

"I saw trolls running from where I found him. When I flew above."

"You expect me to believe that? We would know if there were trolls in our territory!"

"You can believe what you want, but I'm telling you the truth!" I held my ground. "I watched Asante fall from the sky, ran to his side, and found him hurt. For the first time in years, I shifted into my dragon, and I did that to save him. When I carried him away, I saw those trolls running away."

"Or is it that you're working with the trolls?" Domin seemed to grasp at straws as he shot another accusation at me. "Is that why they visited your side of the island?"

I shook my head. "You're out of your mind."

"No, I think my mind is just right. And it'll be even better once you're locked away."

"That is enough, Domin." Asante's uncle entered the room. "Don't you think you've done enough?"

"Eivek, are you really going to protect her?" Domin scoffed.

"From you, yes."

"She hurt him, your own flesh and blood, and you're saving her from me."

"I did not hurt him." I turned to Asante's uncle. "You have to believe me. That is not something I would ever do."

"No one thinks you did, except this fool."

"I am no fool!" Domin was done with words. He darted around the bed and lunged for me, his hands poised for my throat until Uncle stepped in the way. He swatted at Domin, and the old man fell on his back, yelling in agony as his spine snapped against the floor. Just then, Uradis burst into the room.

"Get her out of here, now." Eivek directed Uradis. "It's no longer safe for her here."

I looked at Asante, and as much as I wanted to stay, I knew his uncle was right. It wasn't safe for me there. Domin would have his people after me and he would do everything in his power to convince the others of my guilt.

With no goodbye, I followed Uradis out of the room. She led me directly outside the building. I couldn't help but look over my shoulder to see if we were being followed, but there was no one. Apparently, Domin hadn't had time to get anyone on his side before he approached me.

"You don't believe him?" I asked Uradis as we stepped outside.

"Of course not." She scoffed. "Domin hasn't liked you since the moment you met. And if you ask me, he's the one with something to hide."

"What?"

Uradis looked like she had let too much slip. "Look, regardless of how I feel. It's best you leave."

"Seriously?"

"Yes, Domin has a powerful voice around here. If we want to keep the peace, you need to go while we figure out what really happened here."

"Okay, I will."

"Kiala?"

"Mom?" I turned to the woman who shared my features and couldn't help the smile that lifted the corners of my lips. I'd missed her more than I thought.

"We're leaving. Please, come home with us." My father spoke up, his voice trembling with nervousness.

"What? I thought you would hate me. How can you ask me to come home now?"

My mother ran to me and wrapped me in a hug so tight I could barely breathe. "Oh, my sweet baby."

Confused thoughts flooded my mind. This wasn't the reaction I expected. "How can you hug me after what I did?"

"You're my child. What else would I do?" she tightened her hold. "I'm just so glad you're okay."

"I'm sorry." I buried my face in her shoulder and sobbed.

"We'll talk about this later. For now, let's just go home."

I took one last look back at the door where Uradis stood. She smiled, happy for me even when I wasn't sure I was. After a small wave, I turned away from her and followed my parents to the stagnant dragons that would carry us home. I forced the thoughts of Asante out of my head as I prepared to face the people I'd betrayed when I ran away.

152

CHAPTER 13

Frostspire welcomed me home with open arms. Instead of shame, they met me with fanfare. Just days after my arrival a celebration was thrown to honor my return. Quickly, I realized my mother had spun the story of my absence. I wasn't the daughter who ran away. I was the daughter who lost her way. Part of me wanted to correct the narrative, but I understood why it was necessary. Our internal family issues didn't need to be shared with the world. The royal family needed to look strong.

Especially with the growing threat from the trolls. During the days since I had returned home, my parents filled me in on everything. Trolls were making an impact, threatening both sides. My father clarified that I could never continue my relationship with Asante. Not if I wanted there to be peace between the sides. And we needed the treaty to work if we wanted to survive the onslaught the trolls were clearly planning.

"Are you sure about this?" my father asked. "Once we announce it, we cannot take it back."

"I don't want to be queen." Once again, I declared my true desires. "I didn't before, and nothing has changed. It's not my intention to return and step back into a life I never wanted."

"Are you sure?" My sister entered the room behind me. "This is your birthright as the Promise Born."

I recognized that look on her face. She was poised to say the right thing, but the tightness around her full lips told the truth. My sister wanted me home, but she didn't want me to take over. How hard has she worked to fill my place since I left? How difficult was it to do, mourning a sister while being thrust into that responsibility? Regardless, she'd handled it with grace, like a true queen. Like the queen she was meant to be.

"Leah, be honest with me." I turned to my sister, because the conversation affected not only me. "You've always wanted this, right?"

My sister took a deep breath, collecting herself before responding. She glanced at our parent then back at me. "Yes." The smile lifted the corner of her lips. "I've always wanted this but I was okay with it being you. I trusted you. And even after what you did, I still do. If you want to take your place, I will step aside and allow it. But if you're asking me what I want, it is to rule."

"And you look amazing in this role." I walked over to her and grabbed her hands in mine, tears ready to fall from my eyes. My voice choked as I continued. "Far better than I ever did. Besides, you're going to be married soon. Focus on that, focus on your plans. I'm here, but this is your destiny, not mine."

"How do you two feel about this?" Leah turned to our parents. "Will you allow it?"

"Of course we will." Our father answered, and we both shared a confused glance. "Besides, we need to appear stable to our people and outsiders, especially the trolls. A change in leadership now would make them think we are weak and might encourage them to expedite their plans against us."

"And," my mother nudged his side, urging him to drop the diplomacy for a moment.

"I'm sorry that this was ever something you felt you had to run from," he continued. "We've talked and we realize we didn't give you the space or the choice. This will not be easy to explain to the others, but your mother is brilliant at these things, so I've agreed to let her take the lead."

"I know, and I'm sorry to have put you in this position." I looked at my mother.

"We're just happy you're alright. For so long, I've said you were still alive, and they all looked at me like I was insane. But a mother knows, in my heart I felt you." My mother hugged me. "I'm sorry we made your life so miserable."

"My life wasn't miserable. You gave me a beautiful life and I am grateful for the past, but the future you planned for me wasn't what I wanted. I took the coward's way out and I will forever regret the pain I put you through. But I couldn't think of another way to get away from the fate promised to me by birth."

"It is not a path for everyone." My father nodded. "You're not even the first to want out. My father hated the prospect at first. You are, however, the first to run away."

I dropped my head. Passive aggressive digs were a birthright for him.

"I'm sorry." I said softly.

"No more apologies." My mother clapped and wiped tears from her eyes. "It is time we moved forward and though you are choosing not to be queen, maybe there is something you can help us with."

"Anything, of course."

"I'm glad you're so agreeable because I need you to make your sweets."

"What do you mean?" That was the last thing I expected my mother to ask me. "You spent years telling me to get out of the kitchen and now you're asking me to bake for you?"

"Not for me, specifically." She scrunched her nose up. "We are still hoping to repair the relationship with Starfell. And you won them over in part because of your food and in other because you saved the prince. Your father wanted to keep this away from you, but we received word he is awake, and he confirmed you didn't attack him. Now that's a big relief and I'm happy his parents waited for his account before attacking. Still, the trust has been bent because of your actions."

"I don't understand. Those are typical deserts that anyone here can make." I frowned. "Why does it have to be me when we have a full staff of chefs here who can make them the same? Besides, they'll break down and taste horrible by the time you get them there."

"This is the result of me downplaying your desires for all these years, isn't it?" My mother hugged me, then sighed. "Kiala, you must know there's something special about the things you make. They do not taste the same as others by far. Maybe that was a part of the reason I pushed for you to stop. There was a little jealousy on my side. As for transport, we have ways of delivering our goods, or have you forgotten? We're ice dragons, we can keep them cool enough."

"Jealousy?" My mind brushed right over the rest of her response. "Why would you ever be jealous of me?"

"Because my mother loved to bake. She tried to teach me, and while I picked up the technical side, I could never get them to be as good as hers. You did. If I'm honest, they taste better. They say it's based on the dragon making the food. Each one has a slightly different flavor because of the ice fused with the dessert. Your ice is sweet, and mine was always a bit too bitter for the process."

"Wow, you never told me that before." I stared at my mother in shock. "My ice is sweet?"

"It is. And I didn't tell you because what mother wants to admit to being jealous of their own child? It was my shame. But my shame almost caused me to lose you forever. I won't let that happen again."

"I don't know if I can go back there."

"Not a problem," she paused. "You're not invited."

"Oh,"

"It's not personal. But the relationship between you and Asante was improper." My father asserted. "We don't want to appear as if we encourage that."

"Right." I nodded. "Of course, I understand. I'll do it."

Over the next week, I attended meetings with the leaders of Frostspire. This was my duty. Show my gratitude for their love and appreciation for how they welcomed my return. This was the one time I would be exactly the daughter my parents wanted me to be. Because it meant assuring our people I was not there to return to my duties as the next queen. As my mother put it, after my ordeal, I was in no position to lead, but I was grateful to be home.

Following my mother's lead every step of the way, I had done just that. Everyone seemed happy I was back. No one questioned the decision for Leah to continue in my place. She'd already won them over in my absence.

The morning my parents were to go back to Starfell, I worked tirelessly crafting my best versions of the desserts. I was afforded a private kitchen to work in, one my mother had built the moment we got home. It wasn't finished, but it was good enough to do what I wanted. While I waited for my dough to rise for the fluffer loafs I would make, I pictured what the kitchen would look like when it was done.

"Kiala." My mother entered the kitchen.

"Mother." I turned to greet her.

"You're just as you were when you were a child, you know?" She smiled and glanced at the trays of desserts I'd already finished.

"In what way?"

"You pout when you can't have your way." She pointed at my bottom lip. "That lip was sticking out to the moons. It has been since you returned. I thought it was because you were worried about the decision your father and I would make. We're not forcing you to be our next queen, and yet still you're not happy. Do you not want to be home with us?"

"I'm fine with being back home."

"Fine, but not happy." She sighed. "Perhaps that is because your happiness doesn't live here?"

"Mother,"

"I see it. You are my child, and I know you better than anyone else in the world. That brave face is just a mask. Your heart is broken, Kiala."

"Is it?" I chuckled. "Mother, I'm fine."

"Do you love Prince Asante?" She shocked me with her question.

Stunned, I just looked at her.

"I-,"

"Answer me honestly. There is no judgment here." She reassured me. "This is a safe space, I promise."

"I care for him." I admitted. "But I wouldn't go as far as calling it love. We didn't get that far."

"You care for him, so much that you shifted for the first time in years and risked your own life to save him." She tapped the tabletop with her fingernail. "That sounds like a lot more than simply caring for someone. What do you want to happen?"

"It's not something I've considered." My eyes swelled with tears, but I blinked them away. "It doesn't matter. He has already made his choice. Asante hates me for lying to him, and I can't blame him for feeling that way."

"What if that's not the way he feels? These things can be complicated."

"It almost sounds like you're encouraging something here."

"I would never." She picked up a pastry and bit it slowly. "Better than my mother's."

"Thank you."

"Listen to your heart. You're not bound to stay here forever. Just don't run away without telling me where you are." She kissed my cheek and left me alone in the kitchen.

"Is this a trap?" I raised a brow at her.

"A trap?" she placed her hand on her chest. "How could you ever think I would trap you?"

"Why are you suddenly so open to me coming and going as I please?"

"Kiala, I mourned you. For years. Though I knew in my heart you were still out there, I feared I would never see you again. Now, I can't speak for your father, never could. And you heard him. He doesn't agree with what you did, even though you say the relationship wasn't real. But I will not fight you on the choices you make for your life."

"Will you help me convince him to do the same?" I asked hopefully. I wasn't planning on running back to Asante, but I wouldn't rule out the possibility of going off to start a new life. It would be nice to do so without living in hiding.

"No child," she pulled me into a tight hug. "You're on your own with that one."

A while later, the treats were done and packed in the airtight coolers to insure they would last the ride. I watched as my family flew off, part of me wishing I was going with them. But I understood why I could not. When they were out of view, I did the one thing I could think of to calm my mind. I headed to my kitchen. For hours I worked, baking my delights and when I was done, I stood in front of a large batch of the pastries that were Asante's favorite.

I had intentionally left them out of the order I prepared at my mother's request. What would it say to him if I send his favorites? Would he think I couldn't get over him? Would he interpret it as some message to him? After passing out most of the goods to the aides who worked in the halls of our palace, I headed over to the courtyard. Underneath a blossoming fruit tree, I sat and watched the bird dance as I nibbled on the treats I'd kept for myself. The ones he loved so much. One question echoed in my mind. Asante was awake, but was he okay? I found a seat underneath a full tree and leaned my head against its massive trunk.

It wasn't long before I drifted to sleep with thoughts of Asante as my lullaby. The sound of thunderous wings, the wings of a dragon overhead, woke me. My skin felt hot from the sun, but luckily the shade of the tree I sat beneath had kept my skin from burning.

The fog left my mind just as the dragon landed across the courtyard, knocking leaves from the trees as it did. I squinted against the sunlight as I watched hit carefully. Did I recognize this dragon? Had my daydreaming convinced my brain that he had actually come to my home?

The dragon shifted, returning to true form, and when the dust settled, Asante stood in pants and an open top that showed his chest.

"Asante?" I stood and squinted. When I was sure it was him and not my imagination, I ran to him, slowing to a stop just a few feet away from him. "What are you doing here?"

"You didn't send the jelly ones." He looked at the small plate that sat on the ground where I was. Small bugs covered the plate and the remaining treats he loved so much.

"I didn't." I shook my head.

"Why did you leave?" He took his eyes from the plate to look at me again.

"You told me to." I frowned. "Did you lose your memory when you fell?"

"My memory is fine. But since when do you listen to me?" He fussed.

"You were out of it. I planned to stay until you woke up, but Domin accused me of attacking you. It wasn't safe for me to stay."

"I heard." He looked disappointed.

"But you question why I didn't stay? I heard you cleared my name. Thank you."

"Of course I did. They shouldn't have blamed you at all. Who knows what would have happened to me if you hadn't been there?

And you were right. Trolls attacked me. I saw them just before they struck. I didn't have enough time to adjust my path before I was hit."

"I can't believe they got that far into the territory."

"None of us can," he sighed. "We're still trying to figure out how that happened. It looks like it might be an inside job. I have someone looking into it. Someone I know I can trust. The problem right now is that we don't know how they got in or out without detection."

"I'm sure Domin will figure it out."

"Domin, sure." He hesitated. "Either way, I won't give up until I know the truth."

"Why are you here?" Not that I wasn't interested in what he had to say, but to me, there was something far more pressing.

He chuckled and dropped his shoulders. "That was an abrupt shift in topic."

"Asante, I'm sorry, Prince Asante. I can't stand here and pretend like it's not a big deal for you to be here right now. You said you never wanted to see me again."

"I told you. You didn't send my favorite. Those little jelly filled treats with the sugar dusting." He pointed to the plate. "You won't give them to me, but you will give them to the bugs?"

"You came all the way here for that?" I laughed. "Do you really expect me to believe that?"

"I took you from your home and forced you to live with me for those sweets. Do you think I won't take a flight to see you for them?"

"Right. There isn't anymore. I hate to tell you this, but you came here for nothing."

"And-," he continued. "You. I came here for you."

"Okay, so you *did* hurt your head when you fell." I laughed. "Asante-,"

"Kiala. Do you love me?" He asked me.

"I-," suddenly I felt overheated and like I would choke on the air.

"Do you want to be with me?"

"Asante- this isn't-," I didn't have an answer.

"Don't tell me what's proper or what's acceptable. I'm asking you a question about what you want. That's why you ran away, right? Tired of not getting what you want. So, tell me." He stepped closer to me, and I looked up into his eyes. "What do you want?"

I swallowed the lump in my throat. "Do I have to have an answer to that now?"

"Yes, because you know the answer, you just won't let yourself say it." He grabbed my hand pulling it to his chest. "Say it, Kiala."

"This isn't right."

"Says who?"

"Um,"

"Kiala,"

"I want you to be with you, Asante."

"Good," he pulled me to him and kissed me. When our lips met, the birds sang, the wind picked up, and my heart raced. This was going to be trouble.

"Is this really good?" I asked when our lips parted. "They won't let us be together, you know that."

"They won't have a choice." He grinned. "We're taking control of our futures."

CHAPTER 14

My heart fluttered as I considered his words. How had we gotten there?

From him scolding me about running away from my life to him taking my hand and leading the way. And every fiber of me wanted to do it with him by my side.

"We are?" I smiled, then said in a teasing voice. "Our future?"

"Yes, now," Asante stepped back from me and looked me over. "It's time for you to fly with me, Kiala. Let me see your dragon."

I shifted to my dragon with Asante watching me. When I was done, in full dragon form, he smiled at me.

"Beautiful," he said before shifting into his own dragon once again. And then, together, we took flight.

I followed Asante's lead as he took me to the edge of their territory. I had expected to fly right into their home, but he had other plans in mind. Where we landed, a small convoy waited. Uradis stood at the head of a team of women.

"Princess Kiala. You've returned." She greeted me. "I'm so glad to see you again."

"What is this?"

"I figured you might want to clean up before seeing our parents," Asante answered.

"Smart."

Uradis and her team ushered me into a small tent, its canvas smelling faintly of wood smoke and damp earth, where everything we needed to transform me was laid out. They quickly cleaned me up, styling my hair in an elegant updo and dressing me in a fresh, clean dress.

When we exited the tent, Asante stood with Synth and Kune.

"You look beautiful." He smiled at me.

"Thank you."

"Are you ready?"

"To tell our parents we're committing the ultimate sin? Absolutely."

Synth and Kune carried us right to the field where our parents were. We were just in time to see my parents preparing to leave, but everything came to a halt when Asante helped me down from Synth's back. It was the kiss he placed on my cheek and the image of our hands connected as we approached that caused the first wave of chaos. It was the moment Asante parted his lips that caused the next.

"I am here, prince of Starfell, to let you know, my parents and the council, that I intend to spend my life with Kiala, princess of Frostspire."

The moment he was done speaking, I searched to find my parent's faces. I expected them to be angry, ready to flip out because I had ruined another attempt at creating peace between our people. Instead, they sat there smiling. My mother looked at Asante with a proud look and I stopped to wonder if she wasn't behind it.

Asante tightened his hold on my hand as the gasps and whispers sounded off, followed by the piercing scream from his mother.

"You can't do this!" She stood from her seat. "Are you out of your mind? This is improper."

"This is what I want, mother. I have let you change every part of my life in the chase of filling my brother's shoes." He lifted our joined hands. "This, my relationship with Kiala, is one thing I will not give up for you."

My heart felt like it would burst through my chest as he made the declaration in front of what felt like the entire world.

"What will people think? You are the next king! This isn't right."

"Why are you so concerned with doing what is right when what has been right has left us divided and weak? Trolls are on our shores, emboldened by the fact that we have separated ourselves. So much so that they attacked me. If not for Kiala, I might not be here!"

While Asante argued his point, I looked at my parents. My father looked furious, but my mother had this strange look of acceptance. She said she would support me leaving home, did that support also extend to my relationship with Asante? It didn't matter, because while she may have been leaning toward giving us her blessing, there were three other parents who still looked upset.

"Oh, how wonderful, you're all here." A familiarly annoying voice called out from the trees' edge. We turned to see Domin standing there, partially cloaked in shadows. "This will make things so much easier."

"What is this?" the fire king stepped forward. "Guards!"

"This is me running out of time." Domin lifted his hand and suddenly, trolls materialized from the trees behind him. Their rough, hairy forms loomed around us. "You couldn't die quickly like your brother!"

"My brother?" Asante pushed me behind him as he addressed his former right hand.

"It wasn't easy, coordinating that death and then dealing with anyone who saw what really happened, but I did it. And you were supposed to be just as simple." He clapped his hands. "How perfect was it that you fell for the ice princess? It took so long to find her, and right away, you loved her. All my plans came together so seamlessly. But you didn't die."

"You knew about me?" My chest tightened. "How? I was so careful. No one knew."

"I have eyes everywhere. And when little old ladies owe massive debts, they will do anything to get it wiped clean."

I thought about Mesi, and her knowing looks. All that time?

"We won't waste time now. I am here because it's my time to rule. Your families have destroyed what was once a great civilization. Now we hide from the world, cower away. And how were we to return? A competition? We should be ruling this world, not merely participating in meaningless contests! With all of you here now, that makes my job so much easier. Wipe out the royals and start anew!"

With a defiant yell, he raised his hands, and the trolls, a horrifying mass of claws and teeth, attacked!

Time seemed to warp, accelerating and decelerating simultaneously, a strange and disorienting sensation. The first thing that registered to me was Domin's path for Queen Toci. Instinct kicked in and I ran to cut him off, putting myself in between him and Asante's mother. An action that ended with Domin's fist in my face. It hurt like hell, but the action gave the queen enough time to retreat.

"Kiala!" Asante called out my name. Before I knew it, he was behind Domin. He whipped Domin around by the shoulder and punched him square in the jaw. "Don't you ever touch her again!" Asante continued to pummel Domin. When the man fell slump at his feet, he came to me.

"Are you okay?" He lifted me to my feet.

"I think so. Just a bump, really." I assured him.

"Get out of here, go with the others." He insisted. "I won't allow you to be hurt again."

"No. I'm not leaving you alone." I pointed at the trolls who were still moving it. There had to be at least fifteen of them.

"He won't be alone." Uradis appeared flanked by a mix of ice and fire dragons. The woman was dressed for war.

"How?" I looked around at the collection of warriors by her side.

"I told you I didn't trust that man. He isn't the only one with eyes and ears around here." She winked. "Get to safety, princess."

I allowed the guard to usher me away from the field.

Asante was right.

He needed to focus, and I wasn't a warrior. I complied until I turned back. Asante fought off a troll valiantly but didn't see the one approaching from behind. I tried to break free of the guard who ushered me away, but I was too late. The troll slammed his club right into the back of Asante's head.

"No!" I ran back to the field, fighting off the guard who tried to hold me back.

I tapped into the connection with my inner dragon and pulled the ice power from within. Focused on the back of the troll that threatened Asante, I opened my mouth and allowed that ice to shoot into its back. It pierced the thick flesh. Though it felt powerful, the ice hadn't done much outside of irritating the troll, who turned its attention to me.

The ugly thing took three lumbering steps toward me before Uradis was there. Bold and fierce, she lifted a sword with calculated focus and the troll's head fell from its shoulder. When Uradis nodded at me, I ran to Asante's side. I helped him to his feet.

"We're doing this together." I told him before he could insist I run away again. Fighter or not, this battle was mine as well.

Uradis and her team had already taken out most of the trolls. They weren't our concern. Domin was, and he was back on his feet.

"False Prince!" he cursed at Asante and charged him.

This time I stepped in the path, letting out another blast of ice that Asante followed up with his fist. He fought Domin, exchanging blows as I worked to weaken him with my ice. I wondered why he hadn't used his fire to fight, Domin attempted twice but failed, Asante never did. Then I saw the blood at the back of his head. We had to end this quickly.

I focused my ice on Domin's feet, freezing him from the ankles up, and it worked. The traitor moved slower with each passing moment. I aimed for the final blow of ice that would kill him, but Uradis was there once more. She jumped in between us.

"No, he must pay for his sins! He won't take the easy way out!"

I nodded and stepped back. As Uradis secured Domin, I felt a sense of pride. I hadn't run away. I made a stance. Something I had a feeling I'd be forced to do time and time again if I wanted to truly live the life I wanted. Confident in what we'd accomplished and with the trolls subdued, I turned to Asante. Just in time to see the prince pass out.

While Asante was being cared for, I went to the kitchen. There was nothing I could do, and watching him in his unconscious state only made my stomach hurt. Our parents took off together, suddenly united again on the fight against the trolls. Maybe that would take their minds off Asante and I. Uradis and the other dragons secured the captured trolls who fought by Domin's side, at least those who were still alive.

I returned to Asante. This time, it wasn't long before he woke to find me sitting beside him.

"You're here." He smiled.

"Of course, I am." I placed my hand on his cheek.

"You weren't before." He pulled my hand to his lips and kissed my palm. "I hated myself for telling you to leave."

"I couldn't leave this time."

"The trolls, Domin." Asante struggled to get up, but I placed my hand on his chest to stop him.

"It's taken care of, for now." I told him. "Domin has been captured."

"Good." He sighed.

"I need to ask you something." My heart raced in my chest.

"Anything." He cleared his throat. "What is it?"

"My mother, she sent you back to me, didn't she?"

"Yes." He nodded. "When she got here, she told me about how you talked before she came. She said she only wants you to be happy and though she doesn't completely agree with our love, she gave me her approval to come to you."

"Asante, you're awake." Queen Toci spoke before I could respond to his confession. "Thank you for saving my son's life again, but this doesn't mean-,"

"What my wife meant to say is that we will give you two some privacy." King Sazi spoke. "Budding loves deserve that."

"Buddin loves? I-," Queen Toci ramped up to protest, but again her husband interjected.

"Let's go, my beautiful wife." The king grabbed her hand and headed for the door. "We have far more pressing concerns than this."

"What does this mean?" I looked shocked at the door when it closed behind them.

"It will still be a battle. She won't give up easily and will make your life harder." He raised a brow. "But I think my father is on our side."

"So, she'll be a typical mother-in-law." I laughed. "Can't be any worse than my father. He isn't exactly on board with this either."

"In-law?"

All humor left the room when I realized my slip. "I-,"

"No backing down now!" He grinned. "I want-,"

Just then, I shoved the jelly filled pastry into his mouth.

It was his favorite.

"No talking. It's bad for your injuries." I shook my head. "Just chew and enjoy."

"Shutting me up with food?" he said around the mouthful.

Holding back my laughter, I nodded. "Yes."

"I'm okay with that." He licked his lips and swallowed the food. "There is another way you can shut me up."

"How's that?"

Asante slowly slipped his hand around the back of my neck and pulled me closer to him. "Like this."

Asante's kiss was sweet, like the sugary jelly, lingering on his lips. The familiar flavors of my food were suddenly new and exciting, a symphony in my mouth. A tantalizing mix of savory and sweet moved across my tongue. His lips were burning hot against mine, and his touch sent electric sparks across my skin. I felt like I had finally experienced the reaction I'd seen my customers have so many times before. And I understood.

Our kiss lingered, stretching longer until Asante tried to pull me into the bed with him. But I froze when I felt it again. Just like I had in the cave. Asante's lips shivered against mine.

"Okay," I pulled away from him. "Maybe that's a problem. I don't want you to freeze every time we're together."

"Kiala, you're on fire. Just as you were then, sweating even." He brushed his hand against my forehead and I realized then how my body responded to him. "I should have known something was different about you then, but I was just happy to be with you."

"Is this safe?"

"There's only one way to find out." He pulled me back to him, kissing me again for a moment. "Right now, this is bliss. And that's good enough for me."

"Me too," I kissed him back. We could figure out the complexities later.

As I wrapped my arms around him, I knew that was all I wanted.

I would never let it go.

The end.

ABOUT THE AUTHOR

Jessica Cage is an International Award Winning, and USA Today Bestselling Author from Chicago, IL. As a girl, Jessica enjoyed reading tales of fantasy and mystery, but she always hoped to find characters that looked like her. Those characters came few and far in between. When they appeared they often played a minor role and were background figures. This is the inspiration for her independent publishing journey and the reason she focuses on writing **Characters of Color in Fantasy.** Representation matters in all mediums and Jessica is determined to give the young girl who looks like her, a story full of characters that she can relate to. Jessica has independently published over forty titles and has been featured in twenty different anthologies to date.